Into the

Deep

LAURYN APRIL

Written and Published by Lauryn April
Edited by April Tara
Cover Design by Lauryn April

Contact the author at:
laurynapril.gmail.com
laurynapril.blogspot.com

Thank you to all of my family and friends in supporting my writing over the years.

Prologue

I remember slipping. That feeling when you're falling and you can't catch your balance, your feet sliding out from under you, arms flailing but finding nothing to grab. It's that moment of weightlessness before you hit the ground when your breath catches in your throat. When I slipped, however, I didn't have the ground below me. My bare foot slid on the slick tile that surrounded the pool, gliding effortlessly as if the ground had been coated with oil, sending my body tumbling backwards into Alta Ladera's most elite country club's swimming pool.

I hit the water and for a moment everything slowed. It was as if time had been written on a piece of elastic and was stretched until every number, every minute, was pulled wide and contorted. I could see the look on Damon's face as he lunged forward trying to catch me. I could hear my own sharp intake of breath. I could feel the rush of humid air past my skin. Then the cold water encased me, sucked me in and dragged me down. My hair swarmed out around my face. Like glowing strands of amber backlit by the moon, they spiraled into my view. I remember feeling heavy, and then my head connected with concrete. I heard the sound of my skull cracking against the sharp angle of an underwater step, and then everything went black.

1

Breaking Free

Mom had made juice that morning. She had some fascination with her juicer and would blend up all sorts of vegetable and fruit concoctions. I was grateful to see oranges and not carrots or zucchini on the kitchen counter as I came down to grab a glass before I left for school. Her blonde hair was pulled up into a ponytail and she frowned as I chugged the glass of freshly squeezed orange juice in one gulp.

"Ivy, if you're not going to eat anything, you could at least sit down at the table and drink that," she scolded.

"Sorry Mom, no time," I said throwing my bag over my shoulder. "Thanks for the juice." I left the kitchen before she could reply and rushed out the door in a hurry.

It was Monday, the night before Nicolette Martin had thrown a party at her parents newly remodeled beach house. Everyone had been there. Needless to say, it was busted. I had been down on the beach with Christy Noonan and two of her friends who had graduated the year before. They were USULB students and while I wondered why two college freshmen from Long Beach would want to hang out with two Alta Ladera high school juniors, I had never voiced my concerns. Christy had just introduced me to Steve, a friend of Alex who Christy was currently throwing herself at, when we saw the blue and red lights move down the street. They were accompanied by sirens wailing like a room of dying cats, and had us running as if they were signaling the beginning of a race.

Christy and I quickly discarded our recently opened cans of beer, tossing them with disregard onto the sand, and took off running down the beach. Being the president of the student council, Christy couldn't risk the kind of trouble that came with a drinking ticket, not that it stopped her from drinking. It just made her run faster. That year, I wasn't in any clubs and I didn't play any sports so a drinking ticket wouldn't have affected me any more than the wrath I would have had to endure from my parents.

Christy's blonde hair flew around her face as we ran against the wind. Steve and Alex behind us quickly chugged their beers before following. A ways down the shoreline, we all slowed to catch our breath, inhaling the smell of sea-salt, and laughed at the thought that we'd gotten away. I was just glad I'd been smart enough to park down the block from Nicolette's house since the cops would ticket any cars that were parked right outside.

Alex laughed. "Good thing we decided to walk down to the beach."

"Yeah," I said out of breath. "Good thing."

"We should probably get out of here though," Christy said.

At first I thought she was still worried about getting caught, but then I saw her link her fingers with Alex's. He offered to drive her home and she walked off with him, calling goodbye over her shoulder and leaving me alone with Steve.

"I should get going too," I said.

"Do you want a ride?" Steve asked.

"No, I'm parked nearby."

He nodded. "Well hopefully I'll see you again soon."

I smiled and his eyes lingered on me for a moment. He may have wanted a hug, may have been thinking about leaning in to kiss me, but I was thinking about someone else. I gave him a wave and took a few steps backwards then turned and made my way home. The drive back I was checking my phone for messages every few minutes. I was eager to find out how the night ended for the rest of my friends, those who had been in the house when the cops arrived and especially Christy who left with Alex in his new Mercedes. No one texted me though.

I had gotten a used Scion TC for my birthday a month earlier. It wasn't as nice as Christy's Audi or the Mustang Eliza Hall's boyfriend drove, but I enjoyed not needing to bum rides anymore. I parked it that morning in the student lot, leaving my car in the shade of a palm tree, and made my way into the open courtyard in the front of the school. Christy was already there, standing by the fountain and talking to Tiana Bello. A wide smile crossed my face as I approached them.

"Ivy!" Christy yelled as I neared, "Great news, Steve was totally in to you. He and Alex are coming back down next weekend and said they wanted to make up for our ruined night." Her wavy blonde hair bounced around her face with excitement and her brown eyes were wide.

"Great," I said with less enthusiasm.

"Good, we'll have to go shopping sometime this week then. Ti, you should come with." Christy's eyes locked on the dark-skinned girl looking her up and down, likely mentally critiquing her outfit. That would be something, I would learn, she did quite often. "You don't think your parents are going to tighten the leash on you 'cause of Nicolette's party, do you?"

"Why, what happened?" I asked.

"Drinking ticket," Tiana said rolling her eyes. "Mom threatened to take away my keys until I reminded her that then she'd have to drive me to and from practice four nights a week. That and I told her missing a third of the season of track was punishment enough. I'm just glad she's too stupid to realize that the only reason I took track was as preventative drinking ticket protection."

"How do you know they'll cut you from the track

season and not field hockey?"

"Because Mr. Gutierrez loves me and will totally refuse to not let me play," Tiana said with a grin.

I watched her smile fade after that as her eyes caught sight of someone on the other side of the courtyard. In that moment she looked lost, like her mind was a million miles away from us. Then we heard the loud screech of Mrs. Farrow's whistle. She was the gym teacher, short in stature with short hair and a thin frame. What bothered us most about her was how strict she was. No one ever got a warning from Mrs. Farrow. If she caught anyone doing something against the regulations set in the Alta Ladera High student handbook, she would blow the whistle that hung around her neck as loud as she could and write them up.

At that moment, she was yelling at a group of senior boys who were standing on the sidewalk between the school and the parking lot. They were smoking. I heard her yell something about a tobacco free environment and watched one of them stub out his smoke with the heel of his boot. The boy standing right in front of her however took another drag before putting his out. I stared at him a little longer, he looked familiar.

"Gross," Christy commented, "Who is that anyway?"

"Brant Everett," Tiana answered, referring to the seeming leader of the group who stood with a cocky grin and smiling blue eyes. "The other two are Skyler Bishop and Jason Davis. I have Bio with them, just not very often, they pretty much never go to class."

"Yeah, I think Brant's in my Psych," I said, "usually a no-show."

"Well good, Farrow will finally send someone to the principal's office who deserves it for once," Christy said, still upset about getting sent to the office the week before for having worn a skirt that was, in Mrs. Farrow's opinion, far too short and too distracting to the other students.

"Unlikely," a voice called and we all turned to see Eliza walking up with her boyfriend. Damon Parker had his arm wrapped around her shoulders. Her long black hair was pushed off to one side. "His father's a big shot lawyer who just made a huge donation to the school for a new swimming pool, which I'm totally psyched about by the way." Eliza grinned.

"I'm not," Christy added. "Requiring swimming in gym class should be a crime."

"So should having Phys Ed third period," Tiana said, and I nodded in agreement then looked back over at Farrow writing in her pink slip book while Brant, Skyler, and Jason stood talking amongst themselves. They ignored Mrs. Farrow's shrill voice as she scolded them and walked away from her before she was finished talking.

"So what, he can do no wrong?" I asked. "Hello unfairness."

"Yeah, well, that's how it goes when the school's too afraid to lose its funding," Damon said.

"I so have to convince my parents to donate money for a new pool or something," Christy added.

"Speaking of pools," Eliza said as she pulled something small and metal from her pocket, "I've got the key to the Lakefall Country Club pool house. Anyone feel like going swimming after hours tonight?" Her face lit up with a huge smile.

Even then I knew what everyone was thinking. We would be going swimming.

I never did ask where Eliza got that key as the first bell rang shortly after that. I only knew that she wasn't supposed to have it. Her parents were members at Lakefall and, unless she was required to be on campus with the swim team, she often practiced in the pool there. It wouldn't have been hard for her to swipe the key from an employee; she was good at distracting people. She knew how to flirt, how to get someone's eyes on her, how to bend or move in just the right way. Some poor pool boy had probably been drooling over her breasts while she swiped his key. He wouldn't have stood a chance. She probably could have plucked it right out of his hand and he wouldn't have noticed.

After that, the day dragged on like any other Monday. Math went by easy, but Bio made me want to sleep. Mr. Varnez, who led the Science department, was going on eighty and had a voice more monotone then a sarcastic robot Ben Stein. By the time I got to my last class of the day, AP US History, I was already day dreaming. Mrs. Cole was talking about Abe Lincoln and the Emancipation Proclamation, but I was thinking about Chase Bryant. Daydreaming about accidentally running

into him at the pizzeria where he and the other
football players would often meet up before games. In
my daydream he'd greet me like a close friend, like a
girlfriend, and ask me to join him at his table where,
of course despite having all his friends around, he'd
offer me his sole attention.

In reality, however, I'd never be in the pizzeria at
the same time as him, and if I was he'd never as
much as glance at me. I liked to think I was a pretty
girl, but there were a lot of pretty girls at Alta
Ladera. Chase needed someone who was more than
just a pretty face, and I'd never thought there was
anything particularly special about me. Still, I let my
mind pretend it was a possibility anyway, all the way
up until the bell rang. Then my mind was back in the
land of reality and I started to think about what I
would wear that night to our afterhours swim.

Christy called me shortly after I got home. She said
Eliza's boyfriend had gotten a case of beer from his
older brother before telling me what she was going to
wear. I planned out my outfit as she chatted away on
the other line picking out a green bikini, jean skirt
and white blouse. She was talking about what colors
looked best with her skin tone and I stayed tuned in
just enough to be polite.

I wasn't engrossed in fashion and the latest styles
like Christy. I didn't throw myself into a rigorous
work out regiment to stay competitive in sports like
Ti or Eliza. Sometimes I felt like I didn't really do
anything, like I was just coasting along. I'd like to
think I was just trying to find who I was, but looking

back I think maybe I was just stuck in the in-
between. I wasn't trying to find anything. I was
waiting for something to feel right.

We ended the call agreeing to meet at Eliza's
house at eight and then I finished up the little bit of
Math homework I had before eating dinner with my
mom and sister.

I sat down at the dining room table. Mom came in
from the kitchen carrying a dish of scalloped potatoes
and set them out.

"Sadie," she yelled calling for my little sister,
"time to eat."

She took her usual seat across from me. There
was a place set for Dad as well, but he wouldn't be
making it home in time to eat that night. Mom had
mentioned earlier that he'd be working late for some
big business deal he had going on, but I had paid
little attention. I was used to him missing meals. He
was the CFO of a local insurance company and
seemed to always have an overabundance of late
night work.

Sadie entered the dining room then. She was
eight and had dad's big blue eyes. Mine were green
like Mom's, but Sadie had Mom's blonde hair. She
was quite cute, with her hair in pig tails and
butterfly barrettes, but she was at the age where she
asked a million questions and often demanded
attention. Lately I felt that she'd been pestering me
more than usual, disrupting me when I was on the
phone, or insisting to watch her cartoons when I had
a show on. In middle school, I used to babysit her

every other weekend, when Mom and Dad would go out. We'd sit around and play games, like Go Fish or checkers. Sometimes, I think she just missed spending time with me, but I didn't have the time to give her, and Mom and Dad didn't go out much anymore.

"So, how was school today?" Mom asked me.

"Fine," I replied.

"You have a lot of homework?"

"Nope, got it all done already. Christy, Tiana and I are going over to Eliza's at eight."

"Oh," Mom said disappointed. "I was hoping we could have a movie night. I've got that new romantic comedy, the one with Ashton something."

Mom and I used to have a movie night almost once a week. Usually just the two of us, but sometimes Sadie and Dad would join us as well. Before my junior year of high school, we used to do a lot more together. Spending time with her had become just another thing that had faded from my life, like playing games with my little sister.

"Kutcher."

"Right, right... I was thinking maybe we'd stay in and watch it."

Mom looked hopeful to spend some time with me, and later there would be times when I wished that I had taken her up on her offer, times when I would wish that I had never gone to the pool that night. But I did.

"Maybe we can do it this weekend," I said, "Christy and I are gonna go over our notes for

Spanish. We've got a test tomorrow."

"If you've got school work, I understand," she said with a smile, but I could tell she was disappointed by the tone of her voice. It was too even, she was too calm. "I'm glad you girls are studying together, you learn better that way."

I nodded in agreement and bit back the twinge of guilt from lying.

I got to Eliza's at 8:05. The sun had set hours ago and a hazy sky hung above me. The stars were faint with the city lights stealing from their luster, but a near-full moon left the soft clouds above glowing. As I pulled up, I saw Eliza and Tiana leaning against Eliza's mom's silver sedan in the open garage. Damon was carrying a 24 case of Bud Light from the fridge in the garage to the trunk of his mustang. I parked, leaving room for Damon to back out, and got out of my car.

"Hey," Damon said with a smile as I approached.

"Hey guys," I replied.

Damon shut the trunk then moved to stand beside Eliza but kept his eyes on me.

"We were just talking about the winter formal," Tiana said.

The formal was still months away but I wasn't surprised to see them planning already.

"Damon and I are getting a hotel room," Eliza added. "If we all chipped in we could get a suite, they're like condos practically. We'll dance all night and then drink till the sun comes up... or until we pass out, whichever comes first."

"Well there might be more dancing later in the night," Damon added turning to look at Eliza. She blushed.

"You and Ti should think about it, Christy said she's already in. Oh, but the bedroom is already taken, just FYI. You singletons can have the living room."

I cast Tiana a glance and from her not-so-discrete eye roll, I could tell she was as uncertain about this plan as I was. But before I could say anything, Christy's black Audi pulled up.

"We'll talk later though," Eliza said as she raced over to Christy.

Damon followed and I turned to Tiana.

"That girl is trouble," Ti said and I nodded in agreement.

We watched as Christy parked and got out to talk to Eliza. It was then that a passenger exited the car. I looked on as the pale moonlight made his blonde hair gleam in the darkness. Chase Bryant shut the car door. I felt Tiana watching me as my eyes went wide and my heart started to beat so hard that I feared its sound would echo down the block for everyone to hear.

He shook his head knocking his dark blonde hair out of his eyes. I was so lost staring at him that I couldn't move. I heard Christy talking to Eliza, saying that Chase overheard her talking about our late night swim with Tiana in P.E. and invited him along. Then suddenly they were all standing before Ti and me and I shook my head to knock myself back into reality.

"Hey," Chase said as they approached us.

Ti waved to them but I found myself unable to speak. I could only stare at his green eyes and the perfect curvature of his lips.

"Ivy, you ready?" Eliza asked me.

"What? Yeah, yeah, I'm all set."

"Great," Christy said with a smile then turned to Eliza, "We're gonna ride with you guys, okay?"

"No problem."

I turned to Tiana as the four of them got in Damon's Mustang. She gave me a sympathetic look.

"Come on, you can ride with me," she said and I followed her to her car.

"I told her not to invite him," she said when we got a little ways down the road. "We all know you have a thing for him."

I looked at her surprised. "It's that obvious?"

"Uh yeah," she said and I felt my face flush red. I must have looked horrified. "Well maybe not *that* obvious, but we're your friends. We notice these things. You've been crazy about him since the three of us were lab partners in Freshman Bio."

I just nodded.

"Look, don't worry about it, you know how Christy is, she likes to flirt with every tall, dark, and hunky guy that walks by but she never gets serious with any of them."

"Yeah, you're right," I took a deep breath. "You know, sometimes I wish she would get serious with one of them. Then maybe I'd quit getting dragged on so many double dates."

Tiana laughed. "Steve and Alex?" she asked and laughed again.

"Yeah, they're coming back down next weekend or something. God, I just don't care that much, I'm not quite as desperate as Christy."

"Yeah, I know the feeling."

"How come she didn't ask you to meet them anyway? Didn't you guys carpool to Nicolette's party?"

Tiana's cheeks blushed. "I, um...I was preoccupied at the time."

My eyes narrowed in on her. "What does *that* mean?"

She was speechless for a moment. "I... well, okay remember this morning when Farrow busted those guys for smoking?"

"Yeah."

"Brant Everett, remember I pointed him out, dark hair, cheekbones to die for, gorgeous blue eyes, cute yeah?"

I nodded. "Wait, what does Brant have to do with... Oh my God, you hooked up with Brant Everett at Nicolette's party," I nearly shouted and her dark skin turned rosy again.

"Don't tell anyone," she said in a whispered tone as if we were sitting in a church pew, and I could tell there was some embarrassment buried in her voice. "We didn't... we just fooled around, but... Brant's a total asshole. Trust me on that."

"I'm sorry, Ti."

She smiled. "Thanks, hun. Don't worry though, a few beers and a midnight swim and I'll be just fine."

The golf course at Lakefall wasn't gated itself, just the front entrance surrounding the country club. This made it easy for us to sneak in by driving down a side road. We had to be careful nearing the pool house though. The buildings were not only locked at night but there was a security guard that patrolled the grounds as well. In middle school, a group of about ten of us snuck on to the golf course to play ghost in the graveyard only to end up getting sprayed by the nighttime sprinklers and having to run from the guard. Since then, our strategies to sneak into places had improved.

Tiana switched her headlights off, driving in darkness as she parked a little ways away from the pool house. Both cars were left hidden in shadow and away from the main road where we hoped the guard would not be checking during his nightly patrol. Then Damon grabbed the case of beer out of his trunk and wordlessly we walked to the pool house.

We were all on edge, nervously glancing over our shoulders and huddling close together. I heard every whisper of a sound, from the rustling of leaves and shuffling of feet to the quiet chirping of crickets. We were keeping watch while Eliza unlocked the door. I stared off into the dark moonlit green of the golf course. The clean smell of grass and pine invaded my senses as I tried to see if anyone was coming, but the only movement I caught was of shadows dancing in the darkness. Then I heard the click of the door as she twisted the handle and we all hurried inside.

I sighed in relief once the door shut behind us then followed my friends past the front desk and through the women's locker room. We passed the showers and I felt my stomach twist as I saw Chase put his arm around Christy. I tried to think of what Ti had said in the car, tried not to let them bother me. After all, it's not like I'd even said more than a couple sentences to Chase in my entire high school career. There was no reason seeing them together should upset me. But it did.

We all passed through the glass door that led to the open pool area and I smiled seeing the water before me. The pool was outside but there was a tall brick wall that surrounded it on all sides so we were safe from the sight of any passing security guards. The water was still and reflective as glass. It looked black in the night and shined back the white light of the full moon above. For a moment the wind held its breath and the mirrored water before us looked like it was set in a photograph, a serene and tranquil unmoving image.

"What are you guys waiting for?" Eliza asked. She was running toward the water. Already stripped down to her swimsuit, she did a cannonball into the pool. The water splashed up around her and sent ripples circling out from where she broke the surface.

Then Damon was throwing Chase a beer and Tiana and I were following after Eliza, jumping into the water. Christy hung out with the guys for a little while, sipping on a Bud Light before joining us in the pool. Shortly after that, the boys jumped in as well and we spent the next half hour swimming away from them as they tried to catch and dunk us. Chase mostly swam after Christy but Damon picked me up once and threw me into the deep end. I ended up with water up my nose, but I popped up out of the water laughing.

I pulled myself up out of the pool and sat at the edge with my feet dangling in the water for a short while after that. A moment later Tiana joined me and we watched Eliza and Damon take on Christy and Chase in a game of chicken.

"Well, I'm ready for a beer," Ti said and got up to walk to the other side where the rest of the Bud Light was sitting.

"Yeah, me too."

I followed Tiana and she handed me a beer. The can was wet with condensation and slipped a little in my hand. As I popped the top of the cold aluminum can, Eliza splashed into the water as Christy and Chase won the game of chicken. I took a sip and watched as Damon pulled himself out of the pool. He walked over and grabbed a beer. I was facing him and Tiana at this point and had my back to the pool. The shallow end, only three feet deep, was behind me.

"Hey, Ivy!" Christy called from the water.

I stepped back turning to face her. I didn't realize how close I was to the edge of the pool. I didn't realize that as I moved I would set my foot down and my heel would be over the edge. Christy was in the deep

end swimming toward the ladder and I heard her say
something else, but by then I was falling. My balance
was lost and I slipped, tumbling backwards. That
was it, that one small moment. Just Christy calling
my name, just a wrong step, a small slip, and my life
was forever altered. I couldn't help the way I hit the
water, couldn't have adjusted the angle of my body. I
barely had time to take a breath before I was
submerged. I couldn't have done anything about how
my head hit that last step at the bottom of the pool,
the way I crashed into its sharp edge. The water
didn't break my fall as one would hope, but it did
seem to break something. Or maybe it broke
something loose.

2

Head Above Water

My chest heaved as I tried to find air but only came
up with water. I remember feeling hands on my
chest, and lips hovering above mine. I remember
murmured voices that sounded like I was hearing
them from the end of a long tunnel. Someone said
something about blood, someone wondered if I was
dead. I heard it all clearly but the words were distant
and had a strange ring to them. I wheezed and jolted
upward finally finding my breath and my eyes
popped open. I saw Damon hunched over beside me,
looking frightened, his eyes wide, mouth curved down
into a trembling frown. He moved his hands back to
his sides. There was an audible gasp and I looked
around to see all my friends above me looking on
with concern. I had fallen, I had nearly drowned.
Damon had pulled me from the pool and I could still
feel soreness on my chest where he'd pressed against
my ribs to preform CPR.

"Ivy, are you okay?" Tiana asked.

"You scared the hell out of us," Eliza added.

Christy remained silent. When I looked to her, I saw her arms were wrapped tightly around herself and her eyes were cast at the ground as if they were tied down to something heavy.

I sat up and Damon helped me to my feet, my hand instinctively moved to the back of my throbbing head. There my fingers found a mass of hot, wet tangled hair. I felt dizzy and my head was spinning. My eyes caught Chase's and the intense glare of his green eyes made me look away. That was when I saw the puddle of an oily black substance on the cement where I'd been laying. As I glanced to the pool, I saw a smoke-like gray color swirling in the water. I pulled my hand away and looked down at my fingers. They were coated with blood.

"You with us, Ivy?" Christy asked. "You look like shit."

I looked to her. She may have snapped out of whatever daze she had been in, but I felt like I was slowly falling away from reality. My head felt heavy as if my brain were swollen. It felt as if it was a sponge that had soaked up all the pool water and now sat engorged balancing on my neck, and I was bleeding.

"Ivy?" Damon then asked.

When I looked to him, I found that, despite the pain, I could focus. "Yeah, yeah I'm fine I think."

"Thank God," Christy said, "I so didn't want to have to call an ambulance and explain what we were doing here."

I did my best not to roll my eyes at her and then we heard it. The not so distant sound of a car pulling to a stop, and then the main pool house door opening and clicking shut.

"What's that?" Ti said and we all turned to look toward the pool house. Then the light inside flicked on.

"Shit, it's the security guard," Eliza said, "We've got to go."

"Go where? We can't get back out through the pool house," Chase said as we all scrambled to gather our things.

No one bothered to wonder what the guard would think about the blood, not even me. I had my clothes in my arms and was slipping my shoes on when I heard the grating sound of metal being dragged across concrete. I looked up and saw Eliza pushing one of the small round tables up against the brick wall.

"Come on, we'll go up and over," she said and we all froze, unsure if that was the best way out. "Anyone have a better idea?"

None of us did. Eliza climbed on top of the table, throwing her clothes over the wall. She was the first to jump over and the rest of us followed. Once we reached the cars, I was revisited by the dizziness that had overcome me moments earlier. The rush of adrenaline from the fear of getting caught was wearing off as I sat in the passenger seat beside Tiana. For a moment my eyes fluttered shut and I worried that I'd lose consciousness. Tiana glanced at me. Her normally plump lips were a thin worried line, her eyes wide and unfocused. She was shaken.

"You alright?" she asked.

All I could do was nod yes, but it was only to calm her. I wasn't alright. The entire ride back to Eliza's, I fought to stay awake. My hand held the back of my head tightly as if I were trying to hold it together and, in my mind; I felt like that was exactly what I was doing. I feared my head was cracked apart and that my skull would be in pieces. I didn't know then that it felt worse than it really was, only that a part of me still wondered if I would live through this.

When we arrived at Eliza's I realized that I had blacked out for most of the drive. It seemed as if from the time I got in Tiana's car to the time we pulled into Eliza's driveway that only seconds had passed. I shared this with no one.

Everyone circled around me as I staggered out of the car. Damon was quick to grab my arm and help me over to a lawn chair in the back of the garage. At the time, I assumed they were concerned for me, and maybe to some degree they were. Later, however, I would come to realize that they were all far more selfish than I once thought. Looking back, I can tell they were more worried about getting in trouble themselves. Someone should have called an ambulance. Someone should have called their mom or dad. I should have gone to a hospital. Maybe if that had happened I wouldn't have been left with any... residual effects.

The girls were flustered and completely unaware of what to do. Damon was eager to help me but didn't know what I needed. It was Chase who took control. As for me, my eyes moved around the dimly lit garage, seeing everyone in a surreal, spacey haze that reminded me of looking through a kaleidoscope. Chase grabbed my head and forced me to look at him. He didn't say anything, just stared into my eyes.

"I think she has a concussion," Chase said, his words echoed in my head. Then he turned away from me.

They were all chattering now asking one another what they should do.

"I'm fine," I said, though I didn't know why. I think mostly I just wanted them to stop talking. Their voices were making my ears ring.

Time flickered away from me for a moment then because the next thing I was aware of was Damon and Chase rinsing the blood out of my hair and parting it. The wet strands resisted being separated from one another and tugged against my scalp. I winced in pain. I also noticed that sitting in my lap was a first aid kit and my fingers gripped the corners of the white plastic box.

"My older brother cracked his head skateboarding when I was twelve," Chase said.

I found his voice soothing.

"I went with my mom and him to the hospital. All they really did was staple the back of his head and give him Tylenol, just Tylenol, said he couldn't take Advil, or aspirin... Here, hold that in place."

I think he was talking to Damon and I felt hands on my head then a cold liquid. Later I would realize that they used skin glue to seal up my wound.

"It's really not that bad," Damon said. "A lot of blood, but it's not really wide or deep."

"We really don't need details," Christy said.

Soon they were done and helping me stand. I thanked Chase. He smiled at me and I felt lightheaded for a whole new reason. After that, Tiana was insistent that I couldn't drive home and I watched as they talked amongst themselves. Even now, looking back, they seem dreamlike, their voices distant and resonant, their images fuzzy and glowing. As they talked, I felt like I wasn't really there. I was an onlooker, an outsider. Eventually they came to a consensus and Tiana drove me home in her car. Damon followed in my Scion and they dropped me off waiting until I walked up the front steps to drive away.

At a little past ten, I walked through the front door. My hair was still wet but I'd pulled it up into a pony tail and thrown my shirt and jean skirt back on. I still felt dizzy and there was a bump forming on the back of my head beneath the glue that held my skin together. But that was of little concern to me after I walked through the door. I could hear Mom in the kitchen. She was talking to someone on the phone then hung up as she heard me close the front door.

"Ivy?" she called and I could tell she was upset with me.

I saw her come around the corner and for a

moment she looked at me with relief. Then her eyes grew darker and I saw the corners of her mouth curve down in disappointment.

"Ivy, where have you been?" Her voice was firm and for a moment I didn't know how to respond. "Don't give me some lie about studying. I just got off the phone with Mrs. Hall and she said you girls were out all night. I want the truth, Ivy."

I closed my eyes and took a deep breath. The surreal haze that had taken over my vision before faded and my mom stood in front of me with sharp, bright intensity.

"I'm sorry, you're right. I lied to you."

She seemed to calm a little with my honesty. "We, um, we went for a swim."

She looked me up and down and took in my wet hair.

Then my honesty went out the window. "At the Pool at the Y. We were going to study, but Christy had guest passes that were going to expire today."

Mom sighed. "You should have told me the truth, and I'm not too happy about you girls going out on a school night," she sighed again and I could tell her anger had deflated some, "but I'm glad you're being honest with me now."

I cringed a little inside knowing that I hadn't given her the complete truth.

"Just... go to your room."

I nodded and made my way upstairs. That night I slept terribly. At first I think I'd been afraid to even fall asleep, and after that I kept waking up every few hours. I had a restless and dreamless sleep and found myself the next day with a pounding headache and stiff neck. There was still a large bump on the back of my head from where I hit the bottom of the pool, but I wasn't bleeding and I was still alive.

Mom gave me her *I'm watching you* eyes as I came down for breakfast that morning but didn't give me any more grief than that. I took two Tylenol before I left for school and hoped that my headache would clear up before I needed to do anything that required actual thinking. To my dismay, my head continued to throb all through Spanish, Art, my lunch hour, and into the first half hour of Psych.

I sat in Psych with my head down on my desk. Mrs. Rochester was writing on the white board. Her dry erase marker squeaked as she dragged it across the board with too much force and I squeezed my eyes shut. The noise rang in my ears along with the high pitch shrill of her voice. My headache intensified. For a moment, the throbbing pain seemed to encompass my entire skull. My fingers coiled and twisted in my hair as the pain felt like fire crackers exploding inside my cranium. For a fraction of a second, the pain was so intense that I thought my skull would split straight down the middle, that it would explode, raining brain matter on all of my classmates. Then, just as quickly, the pain vanished completely. I cautiously uncoiled my fingers and opened my eyes, fearful that it would return any minute. It didn't. When I looked up, Mrs. Rochester turned around. She had asked a question, but I hadn't heard what it was, and by the look on her face she was scanning the room to pick the perfect victim to answer it.

"Ivy Daniels," she said, of course, and I faltered.

Then from behind me I heard someone say "The hypothalamus." I glanced over my shoulder but couldn't tell who'd offered the answer up for me. I looked back at Mrs. Rochester, expecting her to thank the person who had answered and at the same time remind them that they were not named Ivy. But she said nothing. She appeared as though she hadn't heard anyone say anything at all and was staring at me expectantly.

"Well, Miss Daniels?"

"The hypothalamus," I said and she turned back around to the board and continued to teach, seeming satisfied that I'd answered the question correctly.

I took a deep breath and ran a hand over the bump on the back of my head. The pain had just stopped, not eased away or slowly faded. It abruptly stopped. I remember thinking all of this a little odd at the time, but I dismissed it. I was just glad my head was no longer hurting.

3

As Real to Them as I am to You

A week later, I was sitting with Christy and Tiana at lunch. My sunglasses rested on my head, their black frame holding back my hair. We were outside on the common, sitting at a round stone table near the fountain. It was a bright cloudless day, but we sat comfortably in the shade of a palm tree, its feathered leaves creating striped shadows on the ground. I was poking at a chicken Caesar salad, pushing the lettuce around with my fork, when I heard Christy say that she'd kill for a Twix bar.

"Yeah, me too," I agreed.

"You too what?"

Had she forgotten what she'd just said? "I'd kill for a Twix bar."

"I was just thinking that too. They really need to fix the vending machine." She took a bite of her apple and I stared at her oddly for a moment.

Then I heard Tiana's voice. *Like you'd really eat a*

Twix bar, Miss Psycho calorie counter, she said. Except I was staring right at her when I heard the words and she hadn't voiced them. She had been chewing a bite of her peanut butter and jelly sandwich the entire time. Still, I knew I had heard her.

"Did you just say something?" I had to ask.

Ti looked at me strangely and swallowed her sandwich bite. "What?"

My mind felt like it was racing, had I just imagined it? "Nothing," I said, "I have to go."

Abruptly, I got up, grabbed my plate, and rushed from the table, leaving my friends sitting alone in confusion. I threw out the rest of my salad without a second thought and went inside. I practically ran to the nearest ladies room and went straight to the sink. I stared into the mirror and turned on the faucet. Splashing water on my face, I tried to calm down, and then I set my sight back on my reflected image.

"Get it together, Ivy. You're hearing voices," I said as I looked into the reflection of my green eyes. "And, now you're talking to yourself too." I sighed, and ran my hands through my hair.

This was ridiculous, I laughed, realizing that I had to have imagined it. Taking a few deep breaths, I convinced myself that it was nothing but my imagination.

The bell rang shortly after that and I went to my next class, Psychology. I took my usual seat at the far end of the room, three seats back. Mrs. Rochester was already writing on the board. I looked around as the rest of my classmates filtered in. My nerves were still feeling frayed from thinking I was hearing voices, but I was calm and shook off the thought. I was tired and the bump on the back of my head from my near drowning accident had essentially gone away but the memory of it remained. I concluded that my odd experience was simply a result of fatigue. That was until I heard something again.

Fuck detention, the male voice practically yelled, but I looked around and could tell that no one else had heard it. You couldn't go around saying the 'F' word at Alta Ladera, or probably any other high school for that matter, without getting sent to the principal's office. *I wish I had a smoke*, the voice said again and I looked to my right to see Brant Everett slump into his seat.

He looked tense. I watched as his fingernails lightly scraped across his scalp and his eyes rolled up to stare at the ceiling. He was twitchy, almost as if he were fighting the cravings of nicotine addiction. He skipped this class often and the look on his face made him appear as if he didn't want to be here now. I wondered if maybe he'd gotten caught smoking on campus again and had been forced to go to class, or maybe he'd been given detention for all his absences. Could what I heard have been his thoughts? Had I been hearing Christy and Tiana's thoughts earlier? It sounded completely crazy. Brant looked at me then and it jostled me from my musings. He caught me staring and his frosty blue eyes narrowed in on me. I looked away.

Mrs. Rochester turned around, finished with her whiteboard notes for the moment. I saw her notice Brant in the seat beside me.

"How nice of you to join us today Mr. Everett," she said.

"Pleasure," he said smugly.

I looked up at the board then and my heart began to thump like the foot of frightened rabbit. Today's subject of interest was written in caps in bright red marker, *Schizophrenia*. It was underlined. Beneath it was a bulleted list of its key symptoms: Delusions, Paranoia, and finally the last point on the list, Hallucinations, seeing or hearing things in which others do not experience. I felt my stomach twist and began to wonder if I was truly losing my mind. People can't really hear other people's thoughts, but some crazy people think they can. I slouched down in my seat and listened intently as Mrs. Rochester started her lecture.

"I thought we'd delve into a little abnormal psychology today. Now, schizophrenics will tell you that the hallucinations they experience are just as real to them as I am to you. While the cause of schizophrenia is often under debate we do know that it tends to occur in people during late adolescence or early adulthood. Also, we tend to see that hallucinations are worse when a person is under stress..."

I started to zone out as Mrs. Rochester continued. I felt like I had just gone down a check list of my own and marked every box. Are you between 15 and 25? Check. Have you recently been under stress? Check. Are you by chance hearing voices that are not really there? Big check.

This class bites, I heard someone say and it rattled my thoughts.

I looked to my left and saw Timothy Nelson put his head down on the desk. I didn't know what to think. Was I seeing into other people's minds or was I losing my own? I focused my attention on every word Mrs. Rochester said after that. Focused so hard I hoped that nothing but her voice would enter my mind. I didn't want to hear anymore voices, and at least for the rest of Psychology, I didn't.

I was supposed to go to two more classes after that, but instead I did something I'd never done before. I left school, skipping the remainder of my day. I had walked in the opposite direction of my next class and went outside onto the common. From there it was a short jog to the parking lot and the school security guard was nowhere in sight. As I neared my car, I saw a puff of smoke float up from around the side of the building. I paused for a moment. Then my sunglasses slipped from my purse and fell to the ground with a clank. I picked them up, and stood as blue eyes emerged from around the building. More smoke drifted up to the sky. I gave Brant a glance then continued walking. Neither of us said a word to each other, but I could tell he was watching me as I made my way to my car.

For some reason I never got a call home about my missed classes that day. Maybe, because it was the first time in my life that I'd ever skipped a class, someone had decided to let my punishment slide. It was only study hall and gym that I missed anyway. Those shouldn't really count as classes. It was possible my absence had simply gone unnoticed. For whatever reason, I was just glad that no one had informed my Mom and that by the time she got home from work, she was over my lying to her about swimming the week before.

Mom worked part-time as a real estate agent so she had somewhat irregular hours. She didn't work every day, but she tried to always be home by 5:00 when she did. When she got home that day, I watched her set her brief case down on the kitchen counter. She said hi and asked her usual questions about how my day at school had been. I was sitting at the island, eating a blueberry muffin, and told her it'd been fine. I didn't tell her that I'd skipped classes, didn't tell her that I'd been hearing voices. I wanted to forget everything that had happened earlier and pretend that it had all just been a dream. I still hoped then that I could escape it.

"What should we have for dinner?" Mom asked me as she opened the fridge. "Your father's going to be home early tonight." *Maybe I should pick up some steaks,* I then heard her say in my mind.

I shook my head and squeezed my eyes shut. I worried schizophrenia was starting to take hold of me, that soon I wouldn't know what was reality or a delusion. Or something impossible had happened and what I was hearing was really other people's thoughts. I didn't want that either. I didn't want any of it, but I decided that I did need to know what was happening to me. Seeing as I wasn't just tired and imagining things and that I was unable to will away the voices I kept hearing, I needed to know what they were. Was I crazy, or was it something more?

It was then that I first started to try and hear the voices, my first attempt at controlling what I would later come to consider an ability. I needed to know if I was really hearing something or if this was some psychological disorder setting in. The one thing that kept me feeling that it wasn't schizophrenia was what I was hearing. Maybe I was being stereotypical and naïve on this thought, but I had expected the voices that I heard to be malevolent if I were suffering from some disease. Honestly, I would have expected them to tell me to kill someone. And maybe that's only what happens in the movies, but the fact that I was hearing things that sounded like the voices of people I knew. I was hearing things that sounded like *thoughts*, that kept me thinking that this was something... else.

Ironically, however, after a day of trying to keep the voices from entering my head again, it was when I tried to listen for them that they vanished completely. I didn't hear my mother's voice as we talked about dinner; didn't hear Sadie or Dad when we all sat down to eat. I didn't hear another sound. That night, not hearing them had been almost as

maddening as hearing them in the first place and I
went to bed exhausted with frustration.

4

The Cards You're Dealt

Friday classes alternated every other week. The week prior I had had my Monday/Wednesday classes which meant I had my Tuesday/Thursday classes to look forward to that day, and I did look forward to them. After a long deep sleep, I woke ready to try and test my ability to hear the voices that the day before were invading my mind. I wasn't sure exactly how I was going to do it at the time, but I knew I had to start hearing them again.

My first class that day was Spanish. Christy was in my class and being around her quickly proved useful. It would be my first insight into how vain her mind really was. I was already seated at my desk when she entered and I heard her the moment she walked through the door.

Why learn Spanish? We live in America. It was most definitely Christy's voice and I looked over my shoulder to see her walk in. She took her seat beside me and said hi.

"You know, I was thinking, why do we need to learn this anyway? I mean, what? 'Cause there's so many illegal immigrants now that we need to all know how to talk to them? This is America, they should learn English."

I laughed and nodded even though I didn't agree with what she was saying. Spanish was a hard class, but I took it because I liked the idea of being bilingual. Christy took it because it was required for the college she wanted to apply to. Christy and I may have both been honor roll students, but I don't think she enjoyed learning the way I did.

"I think they're trying to force us to be well-rounded or something," I replied.

"Well-rounded is overrated." *I should have taken French,* I heard her think. "I should have taken French," she then said aloud.

The weird dèjà vu moment was almost enough in itself to convince me that what I was hearing was really her thoughts. Moments later, however, our teacher arrived and I didn't hear another voice until lunch.

God, look at her tits in that shirt, I heard someone think as I walked down the hallway, passing a group of guys on my way to the common. It startled me and made my head jerk back to look at them. One of them winked at me and I picked up my pace pulling my jacked tighter around me. I pushed past the glass door that led outside and was calmed by the smell of fresh air and the feel of a cool breeze on my face.

Christy and Tiana were already sitting in our usual spot near the fountain, the sound of the cascading water drowning out the conversations of the tables around them. As usual, Eliza and Damon were getting lunch off campus. Today they'd be at *Toppers* as Damon had wrestling practice later. He always got *Toppers Stix* before wrestling.

Only seniors were allowed to leave for lunch, but they didn't keep close tabs on anyone. It was easy for a junior like Eliza to get away with eating lunch with her senior boyfriend. Sometimes they would stay and eat with us, but not often. Getting away from school and fast food were hard to pass up, and I think Eliza enjoyed getting away with breaking the rules.

"Hey, Ivy," Tiana called.

"You ready to hang with Steve and Alex again this weekend?" Christy asked.

I looked at her oddly for a moment. I had thought she'd forgotten about Alex after seeming to be so into Chase only a week or so ago.

"Um, yeah," I responded trying to sound excited. Christy didn't notice the fakeness of my interest, but I saw Tiana roll her eyes beside her.

"Great, I'll call you later with details." *That color green really looks terrible on her; I hope she doesn't wear that on Saturday.*

I tried not to narrow my eyes on her after I heard her bitchy afterthought.

"So what are you going to wear tomorrow?"

I bit my tongue. "Not sure," I said, "maybe that dark blue dress I have." She nodded.

Well, that doesn't look great on her but it's a step in the right direction.

"Hey, Ivy, do you have that Math homework that we got on Wednesday figured out?" Tiana asked me.

"Yeah, mine's all done."

"You mind helping me out with some of it one day this weekend? I'm stuck on number seven."

"Yeah, no problem."

She smiled grateful, but then I saw her look off into the distance. She suddenly had a distracted expression on her face, her mouth falling into a slight frown, her eyes deep and sad. Christy didn't notice, but I followed her gaze to the other side of the courtyard. At first I wasn't sure what she was looking at. Then I heard her.

Smug asshole, she thought, and I saw him.

Brant was leaning up against a tree.

Damn him for being so sexy.

An arrogant smile graced his face and there was a thin brunette standing beside him. The girl, most likely a sophomore, swooned over him as he brushed a stray hair out of her face. I looked back to Ti and she glanced away.

"Well, I'm outta here," Christy said, "Student council meeting. I'll see you guys later." Both Tiana and I said goodbye and then she was off.

I turned back to Ti and caught her glancing at Brant across the yard again.

"You alright?" I asked her and watched her eyes jerk to meet mine.

She blushed as if she'd been caught watching

some racy movie and not just innocently staring at a boy across the yard. She looked at me then glanced back at Brant once more.

"Yeah, I just... It's not like I expected anything with us to turn into a relationship. I guess I'm just thrown by how... nice he was that night. He was a real talker, you know. And then after Nicolette's party it's like I don't even exist."

"He's just a player Ti, just forget about him."

She sighed. "Yeah, you're right."

Even though I could see through to the fact that I was truly hearing voices, doubt still remained like a thin fog clouding my conclusion. I wasn't completely convinced yet that I wasn't losing my mind. I had heard enough that I wanted to believe that what was happening to me really was some kind of mindreading or telepathy, but it was what happened in Psychology that day that persuaded me.

Mrs. Rochester had already written notes on the board when I walked in. Parapsychology was scrawled in blue marker; below it were instructions for an activity. I sat down in my seat and noticed that for the second day in a row Brant was in class and on time. I thought about Tiana's face at lunch and the disdain that she held for him. I didn't even really know him, but thinking about how he'd hurt her feelings made me want to hate him.

"Alright everybody," Mrs. Rochester said gaining our attention, "Since it's Friday, I thought we'd do something a little more fun. Now next week we're going to be diving back into Freud so study up this weekend. For right now, though, I want everyone to partner up with the person next to them. We're going to look at a particular experiment often seen in Parapsychology and I think once we're done you'll all understand why this is a pseudoscience."

I looked to both sides of me to pick my partner. On my left was Timothy Nelson. He was currently sniffling. He looked like he had a cold and was cleaning his glasses with the end of his shirt; not an ideal choice. On the other side of me sat Brant Everett. I turned my desk toward Timothy. He seemed surprised, but said nothing. The rest of the room partnered up and then Mrs. Rochester was handing out what looked like playing cards, but she was only giving maybe four or five to each group.

"I wonder what we're doing," Timothy said when she handed him our cards. He held them up and we both looked at them. There were five of them. They were black on one side and on the other there was a shape.

"These are called Zener cards," Mrs. Rochester explained. "They were used to test psychic ability, specifically for telepathic communication."

My ears perked up and I looked more closely at the cards. They each displayed a different shape. One was a star; another was a circle, a square, a plus sign and then squiggly lines.

"The idea was if a person could guess with any amount of accuracy what was on the card being held up that they contained some kind of psychic ability. We're all going to test one another today. With your partner, randomly hold up a card so they can't see what it is and have them guess the shape on the back. Do this twenty times each and I expect all of you to record your results. We'll discuss them at the end of the class."

This was it, I thought. This was how I could test what had been happening to me. For a moment I felt myself freeze up, my eyes focused on the cards and I bit my lip. It was scary to think that my thoughts about what had been happening to me could be confirmed. It was also equally scary to think that they wouldn't be. I quickly snatched the cards from Timothy.

"You first," I said and proceeded to test him.

I would hold up a card and he'd guess. It was all very simple. I kept a tally of how many he got right and how many he got wrong. He answered incorrectly much more then did correctly, but still he'd get excited whenever he'd get one right. By the time we did this twenty times, he had only gotten excited over his answer maybe three or four times. Then we switched. I handed him the cards and felt my whole body stiffen with anxiety. I took a deep breath trying to undo the knots that were starting to form in my muscles as he shuffled them. He held a card out to me. I stared at the black back of the card and sighed. I heard nothing. For a moment I felt the frustration start to set in, and then something came to me.

I wonder why they picked squiggly lines. They coulda used like a triangle or something.

"Squiggly lines," I said and his eyes lit up.

"You're right." He marked it down on the sheet and picked another card. *Alright a square, let's see if she gets this one.*

"Square," I said and he flipped the card around to show me I was right.

"Two in a row." *No way she'll get three*, he thought and picked another card, *star.*

I continued to guess right and I could tell that Timothy was starting to get a little freaked out. I didn't stop though. This was my proof, I needed this. If I couldn't guess right then the only other answer was that I was crazy. So I kept listening to his thoughts and I kept guessing correctly. I didn't realize that we'd gone through more than twenty cards. I didn't realize that I'd attracted an audience. I was focused. I was listening.

"Dude, she's totally got ESP," I heard someone say then and I stopped.

I looked around. The groups nearest us were all looking at me. The two girls behind us had their eyes glued to me, as did the two jocks in the row in front of us. I looked behind me and saw that even Brant had noticed and was looking at me like I was some kind of sideshow freak. I felt my cheeks flush with embarrassment and my mind rushed to find an excuse to explain why I could do what I did. All I knew was that I couldn't tell them the truth. I couldn't tell anyone the truth. I may have convinced myself that I wasn't completely nuts, but I wouldn't be able to convince anyone else of it.

"How'd you do that?" the girl behind me asked.

My jaw dropped open and I felt my voice wedge in my throat as if I were choking on my words. I raced for something to say. I looked to Timothy, who was cleaning his glasses again, and it hit me.

I laughed nervously, "I um… I could see the reflection of the cards in his glasses."

"Oh!" the girl said and laughed. So did Tim. "I knew it had to be something. Geez, you had us all going."

"Yeah," I said and looked around. Everyone appeared to buy my lie. The guys in front of us turned back around and so did Brant on the other side of me. Before he did, though, he gave me an odd look and I couldn't help but think that he seemed skeptical of what I'd said. It was then that I noticed his partner, Jenny Richter, had glasses as well.

We discussed our results for the rest of class. No one mentioned mine. Instead Mrs. Rochester pointed out that we all had on average a twenty percent success rating and thus none of us were clairvoyant. My success rating, of course, had been one hundred percent. We talked about different types of extra-sensory perception including telepathy, and Mrs. Rochester was quick to point out that she didn't think any of these abilities were real. I, however, knew differently, having finally been convinced.

The rest of that night I continued to hear people's thoughts here and there. I began to realize that I couldn't control it. It was easy to listen for the voices, but impossible to block them out. I didn't know how, but it hadn't started to bother me yet. Mostly what I

heard were random snippets, like the pieces of
conversation or lyrics you hear when flipping through
radio stations. A girl complaining in her mind about
having to run in gym class, a boy having an inner
monologue about the way some girl's boobs bounced
as she ran. Most of it was trivial, some of it annoying.
In study hall, I listened as someone kept repeating
the chorus to *Another One Bites the Dust.* Even in
their head they sang off key and with terrible
rhythm. At home I heard Mom listing off bills she
had to pay in her mind and Sadie wondering if Dad
would take her to the park that weekend. After
dinner, I spent the rest of my night in my room.
Sitting in there alone I heard no one and welcomed
the quiet. I'd heard enough thoughts for one day.

5

Going Against the Current

On Saturday I wore the blue dress. I didn't care if
Christy only thought it looked *okay* on me. I liked it.
It was a dark royal blue, short with spaghetti straps.
It was simple but it fit well. I had spent the earlier
part of Saturday in my room avoiding the voices that
I knew I'd hear if I went around my family. I called
Tiana and helped her with her math homework then
finished the rest of the reading I had for Lit. By
eight, I was dressed and waiting for Christy to arrive.
She had called around seven saying that she, Steve
and Alex would be there in an hour to pick me up. I
was nervous, not so much for being around
the boys and having Christy push Steve onto me as a
potential love interest, but because I was unsure of
what I would hear. Since coming downstairs I hadn't
heard a single voice, but I wasn't optimistic enough to
think that I wouldn't hear any that night.

A short while later, Alex's Mercedes pulled up

and I got in the back seat. It smelled of leather and cologne, thick and musty, like ginger and fresh cut wood. Steve was sitting in back with me and Christy was in the passenger seat. We were headed to the beach to have a small bonfire and watch the waves roll in. I was expecting a relaxing, fun night. I wouldn't get one.

"So, what do you like to do for fun?" Steve asked me on our way there.

He, not so smoothly, reached his hand across the back of the seat behind my back. I wanted to roll my eyes, but was glad that it was only his outward cheesy moves that had my attention and that I hadn't, at least not yet, heard his inner intentions.

"I mean other than hitting up house parties and going to the beach with handsome guys like us."

I laughed, "Handsome, huh?"

"Oh most definitely. So what do you like? Play any sports?"

"Not so much. I got into volleyball for a while. It was fun, but I never was good enough to make varsity so I gave it up."

"Volleyball, well maybe we'll have to get a game going the four of us."

I smiled genuinely when he said that. I had really liked playing volleyball my freshman and sophomore years, but I liked to play the sport for fun and after a while the long practices and heavy competitiveness that was known of all Alta Ladera sports started to make the game less of a game to me and more of a chore. My friends had never understood why I quit.

To them it was important to be involved in school activities; to me it was about doing what I enjoyed. It was nice to think about playing again just to play. I was starting to feel like maybe it would be a good night.

Once we reached our destination, the four of us made our way toward the fire pit. The dry sand slowed me down as I tried to run along the beach. Christy and Alex were up ahead of Steve and me, working on getting a fire going. Steve was carrying a six pack of Coors Light and I had a bottle of White Zin courtesy of Christy's mom's wine rack. We looked on at Christy and Alex in the distance as they struggled to get a flame going.

"Looks like Alex has forgotten how to work a lighter," Steve said.

"Yeah, they're not doing so good over there." I smiled.

I think we need to get everything heating up a little more around here, I heard him think and my smile faded a little. "By the way, you look really good in that dress," he said.

"Thanks," I replied and couldn't help but smile again, until I heard something else.

It'll look better when I get it on the floor though.

I started to walk with a greater distance between us after that. I barely knew Steve. We'd only met a few weeks earlier at Nicolette's party and he already thought he could... what? Get somewhere with me? It was starting to be obvious exactly what these two USULB college freshmen wanted with two high school juniors.

Christy and Alex had just gotten the bonfire going when Steve and I reached them. Its flames clawed their way up to the sky and cast their faces in orange light. Christy was sitting beside Alex in the sand and he had his arm around her. I hovered uncomfortably for a moment as Steve set down the beer. He plopped down in the sand and I hesitated not wanting to sit beside him. I was out for a fun night with friends and he seemed to want something more and so did Alex.

God this girl has great legs, Alex thought as he eyed my friend.

"Come on, Ivy, sit down," Christy said, glaring at me. *Don't be antisocial, you're going to embarrass me*, I heard her think.

"Right, yeah," I mumbled and sat down between her and Steve.

She snatched the bottle of wine out of my hands with a smile and pulled out the already loosened cork. I heard it pop then watched her take a long sip. Steve leaned across me to hand Alex a beer, and Christy handed me the bottle once she was done. I stared at it for a moment then looked to Christy. Her eyebrows rose and she looked at me with expectation. I took a sip from the bottle.

"So," Alex said, "how about we get some kind of game going?"

"Drinking game?" Christy asked. She beamed a smile at him.

"Oh, Flip, Sip or Strip," Steve said.

"Strip?" I asked in a suspicious tone and shifted

my weight in the sand to pull my dress down over my knees.

"Yeah, well you don't have to strip," *at least not right away,* he added in his mind. "It's easy, you just..." he pulled a quarter out of his pocket. "Flip, call out heads or tails before it hits the ground and if you're right, just pass the coin."

"What if you're wrong?"

"Then you either take off a piece of clothing or take a pull of your girly wine there."

I looked down at the wine bottle in my hand and thought that it might be alright. I had never had problems playing drinking games in the past. I was quite good at beer pong actually.

"But," Alex added, "You can't do the same thing more than twice in a row."

I watched Christy read the look on my face, "Come on, it'll be fun," she said before I could object.

"Alright."

Steve smiled and flipped the coin first. He called out tails and I leaned in to look at where the coin had hit in the sand. It was heads. I watched then as he took a long sip of his beer. He handed me the coin. I tossed it up into the air and called heads. I bit my lip as it tumbled back down to the ground.

God, I hope it's tails. I heard Steve think. It distracted me for a moment. *Damn,* he then thought and I looked down at the coin to see that it was as I had called it.

Christy went next and ended up having to take a pull of the wine which she seemed happy to do. When

Alex was up, he guessed wrong as well but opted to lose his shirt instead. Christy flashed me a pleased look.

Older guys are so much better looking, I heard her think, and then the coin was passed back to Steve.

He guessed right. Then it was back to me.

I hope she starts losing, I heard him think as he handed me the coin, *I've got four girls back on campus that I can get naked in half this time.*

I froze. My hand gripped the quarter as the heat from the fire licked my knuckles. I didn't flip the coin. I didn't want to. Everyone stared at me as I sat there unmoving.

"Ivy," Christy said. "Flip it."

She's not even as hot at Rachel, Steve then thought, *but hopefully she'll be a good lay.*

"I can't," I said and stood up. "I have to go."

Christy's eyes were huge and she flushed bright red with humiliation. I walked away from them and started to make my way back to the parking lot. My feet dug into the soft sand and I clenched my fists so tightly that my nails were digging into my palms. I was hurt and angry, mad at what I'd heard Steve think about me and mad for the fact that I knew what he was thinking.

"Ivy!" Christy called and I turned around to see her catching up behind me. "What the hell are you doing?"

The guys were still sitting around the fire down the beach.

"Christy you don't know... these guys don't care about us... they just..."

"Oh come on Ivy, just 'cause our parents tell us that *'guys only want one thing'* doesn't make it true about all guys. Alex and Steve are really cool, and hot, and if you mess this up for me I'm gonna be so mad at you."

"I'm sorry Christy, I don't feel comfortable with these guys. I'm going home. You can either come with me or stay here, but I'm not staying."

Her face grew rosy again, making her look like a spoiled child being told 'no' for the first time.

"Fine, be lame. I'm going back to the bonfire to do damage control and try to salvage my date. Don't expect me to *ever* ask you out with me again." She turned away from me with a flip of her hair and stormed off back down the beach.

I walked home alone.

At home, I went straight to my room and pulled out my laptop. I needed to know more about why I could hear people's thoughts. Knowing what people were thinking wasn't just interesting or annoying anymore; it was starting to interfere with my life. I wondered on my walk home if my night would have gone better if I couldn't read minds. If I didn't know what Steve had been thinking, would I have found him charming? Would I have stayed and had a fun time? Would I have ended up getting drunk and doing something I would have regretted? I shook my head. I didn't want to be grateful for my newfound gift. I was mad and frustrated at being able to know what people were thinking, but more so I hated that I couldn't just have told Christy exactly what I'd heard. I hated that I couldn't explain why I left the beach.

I sat on my bed; my yellow comforter wrapped around my waist, with my laptop before me and pulled up a browser window. I went to the search bar and typed in *telepathy*. I scrolled through the generated list of web pages and read through a definition as given by *Wikipedia*. I concluded that what I was experiencing was in fact transference of thoughts from other people to me, but that didn't explain why. I went back to the search engine and glossed past links to various superheroes and comic books. There were links to movies and books, entries for New Age self-help books dedicated to 'discovering the inner you' and listings for psychic hotlines. After a few pages of finding nothing to offer me any real answers, my shoulders dropped and I let out a huff of defeat.

I felt like I had been cursed. I didn't know how to control what I was doing, didn't know how to escape it. I had the ability to see into people's private thoughts and yet I felt like I was the one being violated. I felt like I could never again have mystery in my life; never again let people tell me things when they were ready. Everyone around me would be wearing their hearts on their sleeves, they'd be entrusting me with secrets they never told me, they'd be letting me in to their deepest desires and worst fears just by thinking them around me. The ability to judge people not only for who they are on the outside but for the things they think, for the things they keep to themselves, was frightening. I found myself with an ability and a responsibility I'd never wanted and the worst thing about it was that I didn't even know why.

I went back to the search engine and typed in the only other thing I could think to type- *swimming pool accident*. At first I found nothing that really related to what I wanted to know, but I wasn't expecting much. There were a number of news articles about various accidents. Small children drowning when left unattended, a woman becoming paralyzed during a party, but nothing related to acquiring strange abilities after an accident. I tried a different search term. *Hit head on bottom of pool*, I typed. Then I found one article that I thought might help me understand. I clicked on the link and began to read the article. It was about a man who hit his head at the bottom of a swimming pool and woke up with astounding piano skills. Before his accident he'd never even played the piano, but after he was an instant concert pianist. He still can't read music, but he can play it.

I kept reading, feeling for the first time like I wasn't alone. I hadn't discovered another person exactly like me. He couldn't hear other people's thoughts, but he did develop an ability that he didn't have previously, and after an accident nearly exact to my own. I at least felt confident that what had caused my ability to know what people were thinking was my falling into the pool at Lakefall Country

Club. I didn't have all the answers, but I had
something.

6

Into the Deep

On Monday I was the first of my friends to arrive at school. I made my way across the open courtyard to wait for them by the fountain. Leaning against the cold stony ledge, I listened to flow of the water behind me and exhaled a deep breath. After how Saturday night ended, I wasn't expecting Christy to have forgiven me yet, but I knew she would eventually. With the sun warming my face, I closed my eyes and soaked up a moment of peace. I imagined that I was out in the woods, sitting beside a babbling creek. I envisioned camping in Big Sur, where my father liked to vacation. I could even smell the willowy, earthy aroma of the forest. Then my tranquility was shattered.

Well, if it isn't Miss Mind Reader from Psych class, I heard and opened my eyes, except I thought that someone had said it out loud. *Probably a bitch just like Tiana.*

I spun around enraged, and then the words were tumbling out of my mouth before I even had a chance to think about what I was saying.

"I'm not a bitch, and neither is Ti," I said to Brant who sat on the edge of a tabletop a few feet behind me.

His eyes went wide and, then as his blue orbs narrowed on me, I realized my mistake. He stood up and took a step toward me. He wore a dark jacket with a plain black t-shirt underneath and he looked at me with a creased brow and inquisitive expression.

"What?" he asked.

"Nothing," I quickly said, but he wouldn't let it go.

"No, you just said that you weren't a bitch and that neither is Ti... I never called you a bitch," *not out loud.*

"I must have just heard someone else say something... sorry." I tried to walk away from him then but he grabbed me by the arm and spun me back around to face him.

Did you hear me think that?

My lips parted and I almost responded to his thoughts again, but it was at that moment that Tiana arrived.

"Ivy, what's going on?" she asked and I saw her standing only a few feet from us.

Brant let go of my arm then.

"Nothing, was just leaving," Brant said.

He turned and walked away before either of us could say another word. I watched for a moment as he walked across the courtyard to where I could see his friends Skyler and Jason standing. I turned back to Ti.

"He's a dick," I said.

"Warned you. What'd he say anyway?" *Probably was trying to hit on her, that guy has no shame.*

"I just heard him say something rude. Don't worry about it, I told him off."

"Told who off?" Eliza asked.

Tiana and I turned to see her approach. She had her long black hair pulled up into a high ponytail today and it swayed as she walked.

"Steve? I heard you ditched out on Christy on Sat." *And boy was she pissed about it.*

"Oh God, what did she tell you?"

"Christy didn't tell me much, but like half the school is talking about it. Some friends of Steve and Alex said you ditched out on the date, stormed off across the beach."

My cheeks flushed and felt like my skin must have resembled a ripe cranberry.

"Don't worry, from the sound of it, she wishes she would have left with you."

"Guys were dicks?" Tiana asked.

"Big time," I replied. "Is she mad at me?" I asked Eliza.

"Well you know Christy, she'll act pissed that you ditched for a couple days, probably be embarrassed that the whole school knows you left her alone on a double date... and then forget all about it."

I nodded. Christy giving me a hard time was not something I was looking forward to, but I had other, more important, concerns at the moment. Brant Everett was on to my secret and I didn't know what to do about it.

By first hour, I found I had another problem. I was hearing thoughts quite a bit more then I had before, and the overlapping tones of voices were buzzing in my ears. Sitting in math class, I attempted to work through the example problem that Mr. Sumner had written on the board but the thoughts of everyone around me kept me from focusing. Some were thinking the problem through, others were daydreaming. They were thinking about their weekends, movies they'd seen, boys, girls, how Mr. Sumner, who was in his twenties, looked in that argyle sweater. It was as if twenty TV's had been turned on in the same room but were all set to different channels. All of it was immensely distracting.

"Mrs. Daniels," he called on me, "what did you come up with?" I panicked. I hadn't been able to focus well enough to actually do the problem. I gaped at him for a moment and then I heard my salvation.

Nineteen, someone thought.

"Nineteen," I said and he looked almost shocked for a moment but then continued on. I sighed in relief.

Lit went by similarly, and by the end of second hour I found myself with a throbbing headache. I was hearing more and more with every hour that passed. It was one thought after another, a continuous stream that overlapped voice over voice and I didn't

know how to block them out. By the time I got to Bio,
I had a little reprieve. We were watching a movie the
entire hour. It was dated and I was forced to listen to
terrible '80s theme music, but a good number of my
classmates decide to sleep during the film and I was
free, for the most part, of their thoughts.

On my way to lunch I stepped down an empty
hallway and leaned against the wall. I tilted my head
back and started to rub my temples. Alone in the
hall, I had a minute with my thoughts and only my
thoughts; just a minute where I didn't pick up anyone
else's brainwaves. The throbbing of my head started
to ease a little. Then I heard one more.

Ivy's pretty cute.

I looked up. My eyes snapped open. Walking
down the other end of the hallway was Chase Bryant.
My eyes went wide. I hadn't really seen him since the
night at Lakefall Country Club as we didn't have any
classes together. Had he really just thought that I
was cute? For a moment my breath hitched and I felt
my palms grow sweaty as he walked toward me,
shaking his dark blonde hair out of his eyes.

"Hey," he said.

My words caught in my throat. "Hey," I finally
responded.

He smiled at me and I smiled back. That moment
dragged on as we gazed at one another. I was
reminded of when he stared at me in Eliza's garage,
the way he held my head and looked deep into my
eyes. In retrospect, he was only looking to see if my
pupils were dilated, but that moment in the hallway I

remembered it in some romanticized dreamlike vision.

Chase cleared his throat.

"Do you know where I could find Christy?"

"Oh," I said and my smile faded along with my hopes. "Yeah, um, yeah she'll probably be sitting by the fountain on the common unless she has a student council meeting."

He smiled again. "Thanks," he said and walked past me.

I sighed. He may have thought I was cute, but he was still into Christy. I took another minute to myself and then started to walk to lunch. I walked through the doors that led outside, and it was then that it hit me.

It was like a fog horn going off in my ear. I took one step onto the common and squeezed my eyes shut as the pain intensified. I heard it all, thoughts from every student that encompassed the space before me. Hundreds of voices all in my head, all at once, words and phrases layered on top of one another. They sounded like screaming as they jumbled together and grew in volume. The voices were pushing into a space designed for my thoughts, designed for my thoughts alone, and it felt like there wasn't enough room in my head for all of them. It felt like my skull was going to crack open and that my brain would swell until it was the size of a hot air balloon.

My hands reached up to either side of me head and pushed against my ears as if that could keep them out. It couldn't. The voices continued to grow in number and volume and I felt myself getting faint. I couldn't take anymore. My knees started to buckle, my arms fell limp, and then I tumbled to the ground. There were two things I noticed before everything went black. The first was the feeling of arms catching me before I hit the pavement. The second was one clear voice.

A month from now, they'll all be dead.

When I woke, the voices were gone. Well, most of them. I was lying on a thin mattress. My head was still throbbing slightly, though nowhere near as bad as before. The room was hazy and bright when I first opened my eyes. Sunlight streamed in through the window and lit up the tiny particles of dust that floated in the air.

Leaving on a jet plane, I heard a female voice sing. The John Denver tune was recited over and over in her soft voice.

The air was stuffy and humid and it smelled of antiseptic and plastic. I looked around as the room started to come into view and saw I was in the nurse's office.

"Oh! You're awake," the nurse said as she walked over to me.

She was a lean woman with light blonde hair and thin lips. I'd never met her before, as I rarely got sick and didn't tend to like going to the nurse's office. I sat up swinging my legs over the small cot I'd been laying on, and she placed the back of her hand against my forehead. As she checked for a fever, she started to hum the song she'd been singing in her head aloud.

She looks alright, I heard in a familiar voice and looked to my left to see Brant sitting slouched in a chair on the far side of the room. His eyes were locked on me with concern and yet his body language was cool and relaxed.

Pieces of what had happened started to filter back into my mind at that point. I remembered the voices, the pain, remembered how I had felt woozy and spiraled to the ground like a falling leaf. Then finally I remembered not hitting the cement, but being caught in strong arms. Brant must have caught me before I hit the ground and brought me here. He was probably standing in the shadows along the side of the building where I'd come out, maybe he'd been smoking, and then he saw me freak out. He would have seen me wince in pain and bring my hands to my head to cover my ears. I felt my skin blush in embarrassment imagining how strange I must have looked.

"Well, you seem like you've got a bit of a fever," the nurse said. "Mr. Everett here said you took quite a tumble out on the common."

"Um, yeah… I must have fainted… I skipped breakfast this morning," I lied.

"You probably have low blood pressure, and it seems like you've got a bit of a cold coming on. I'm gonna let you go home if you can get a ride-can't let you drive after fainting-but you have to promise me you won't skip breakfast again."

"I'll take her home," Brant said and my head

jerked to face him. "I've got a free period next hour."

"That's very noble of you, Brant, but I'd have to okay it with your parents."

"Actually, I just turned eighteen last week, so I could take her and come right back, you wouldn't have to okay it with a soul."

The nurse thinned her lips and thought for a moment. "Well, alright," she said and turned back to face me. "I'll write you a pass."

I turned to stare daggers at Brant. I didn't know what he was doing, why he was helping me, but I felt like he had to have some alternate agenda.

I stomped down the hall away from the nurse's office. Brant was behind me. I didn't want him to take me home. I didn't want anything to do with him.

"Hey, hold up," he called out and caught up to me.

I didn't slow down. "Look, thanks for not letting me crack my skull open out on the common and all, but I don't need your help."

"Oh really?"

We were still walking at a fast pace and the door leading outside was in view.

"Well, I promised the school nurse I'd take you home, so seems you're stuck with me."

"I don't think the school nurse is going to have any idea if I choose to drive myself home at this point." I had my hand on the door and began to push it open. "So thanks, but no thanks." I stepped outside and he followed me.

She's so damn stubborn, I heard him think and then a second later it was if I was standing before a firing squad and had a dozen pistols shooting at me.

The moment I took a single step outside, the voices flooded my consciousness. I was hearing the thoughts of a few hundred students again. It was the end of the lunch hour and the common was still filled with kids. The pain came next and I winced. Instinctively my hands flew to my head and then I felt Brant walk up beside me. He reached an arm around me and guided me away from the building. Reluctantly I walked with him. The farther away we got from the common, the fewer voices I heard and the softer they got. We rounded the corner and the pain started to ebb. I shut my eyes for a moment, letting him lead me as I rubbed my temples.

Then I heard the car door open. I hadn't even realized we'd stopped walking. I opened my eyes and saw him staring expectantly at me. His hand was on the opened passenger door to the lackluster and rusting '80s Camaro.

"I'm okay now, I don't want your help."

"Yeah, well... I'm all you've got right now."

I glanced back to the courtyard of the school. From where I was standing I was out of range of their thoughts, but I knew if I walked back a few steps, I'd start hearing them again. And, relentlessly, they would pour into my skull. In that moment I felt like an outcast. I felt pushed away and exiled and the loneliness of it was a boundless crater that I'd fallen into to be swallowed up by the darkness. I couldn't go back there, not then.

Just get in the car, I heard him think, and I did.

For a short while after he got in the driver's seat there was silence. Brant didn't say or think anything as he started the car and pulled out of the student lot. I felt relieved for the moment of quiet, and yet at the same time wished he'd give me some clue as to why he was helping me. I wished he'd think something, anything. I found, however, that he was good at keeping his thoughts hidden.

"Where do you live?" he asked.

"Two-twelve Sunnyside Lane... it's down off of Parkway."

He nodded then after a moment's pause, he turned to me. "So, you can... you can hear what people are thinking."

I looked to him but said nothing.

"I mean, that's what that whole fainting thing was about yeah? You were hearing them all at once weren't you?"

Again I was silent, this time looking away from him to stare out the window.

I wonder what it's like, I heard him think then and it brought my gaze back to him.

I decided to answer his question. I sighed. "It's like... it's just like hearing people talk, except they don't know you can hear them."

His gaze shot to me and the car swerved an inch but he quickly regained control. Brant looked at me with a mix of wonder and fear.

You really can hear thoughts. "So you hear everything then, everything people think?" *Can you hear me now?*

"Yep."

God, this is crazy.

"Yeah, you're telling me. Look, this isn't something I'm all that thrilled about being able to do so could we not talk about it right now?"

You don't know how to control it.

It was a statement not a question. This time I chose not to answer.

"You don't, do you? How long have you been able to do this?"

I sighed. "Hit my head at the bottom of a pool about a week ago, nearly drowned, since then I started to hear things… just now and then, but then they got louder and now… I can't stop them."

God, she looks so upset, I heard him think but then he shook his head and hurried the thought away, as if he hadn't wanted me to hear it. "Well, there's got to be a way to do that, to turn it off?"

"I don't know." We were both silent for a moment. "Why are you even here anyway, why catch me, take me to the nurse?"

I wish I knew, "I was just there… when you fell. I was standing out of Farrow's sight having a smoke and you walked out of the building. You looked like you were in pain and then… you were gonna hit the ground, and hard. I couldn't just let you fall."

I remembered something else then, something I heard just before I passed out. A voice had said *A month from now, they'll all be dead.* Remembering it sent a chill through me. I looked to Brant for a second, but I knew the sound of his voice. It hadn't been him. Whoever had said it seemed angry at the world. It was a deep male voice that even in so few words had been filled with pain. I didn't know then what to do with what I had heard, but I did know that whoever had thought it had meant it.

"What are you thinking?" Brant asked and I realized I'd been lost in my thoughts.

"What? Nothing, it's nothing." I saw we'd turned on to my street then, and my house was coming up.

Brant was still looking at me waiting for me to tell him what I'd been thinking about when I zoned a moment ago, but I didn't want to tell him about the voice I'd heard.

"My house is that white one just up the block, the one with the red mailbox."

He looked to where my house was then glanced back at me. "So you're not gonna tell me anything else then?"

I looked at him with wide eyes and a crumpled brow wondering why he suddenly thought he was someone whom I could confide in.

"Brant, I barely know you. Until today you've hardly said two words to me. I realize you have some fascination with this thing I've been cursed with, but… we're not friends."

"Right," he said and then pulled into my driveway and the car came to a stop. *We're not friends, would'a never even have talked to you or any of those stuck up bitches you hang with otherwise,* he thought. "Well, I guess I'll see you around then."

I got out of the car and he sped out of my

driveway. For a moment I just stood there looking out into the road. His thoughts were angry, but he chose to be civil aloud. He seemed like he was conflicted with hating who he thought I was and wanting to get to know me better. It was strange. I thought then about how I had told him that we weren't friends. It was true, but looking back it sounded so mean to say. For a moment I felt bad for having hurt his feelings with those words. Then I remembered that he was Brant Everett. I remembered that he'd hooked up with one of my good friends at a party and didn't give her the time of day after. I remembered that everything I knew about him said that he was a complete asshole.

7

Beneath the Surface

The next day I convinced my mom that I was coming down with a cold and needed to stay home from school. She'd agreed without any argument. I wasn't known for skipping or faking illness and so she assumed I really was sick. And, in fact, I felt like what I was experiencing was a sickness, just not in the way she was thinking. For a moment I heard her worry about me with true concern, her thoughts focused on wondering if this was something serious. I assured her the best I could that this was only a bug and she went off to work leaving me alone in the house.

I slept in a few hours later than I would normally but after that I was up and wide awake. I wandered around my house for a little while, enjoying being alone with my thoughts. I poked through the fridge, finding nothing to eat, and then flipped through the channels on TV, finding nothing of real interest.

Sitting on the couch, I sighed in frustration. I was trying to avoid the real issue that I had. I needed to know how to control this ability that had afflicted me, needed to know how to get rid of it if I could. I didn't think that was possible though. Still, I knew I couldn't hide away in my house for the rest of my life. I had to learn how to live with it.

I felt like my accident in the pool had knocked something loose in me. It had broken down some barrier that kept everyone else's thoughts out, and I didn't think that that barrier could ever be restored or replaced completely. I just hoped that I could learn to close up whatever doorway had been opened, even if only for a little while.

In search of answers once again, I went up to my room and pulled out my laptop. Lying on my queen size bed, I wrapped myself back up in my yellow comforter and pulled up a search engine. My fingers hovered above the keys for a moment and my brain raced trying to think of what to type. I didn't think there was anyone else out there with the same ability I had and my searches the week before had shown that if there were others like me, none of them were advertising on the World Wide Web. I thought about what it was that I wanted. I wanted to know how to block the voices out that I was hearing. I wanted to close the door on them.

Doorway to the mind, I typed and hit enter. At first there was nothing that seemed like it would help. After scrolling past a number of links, however, I found one that talked about opening doorways in the mind. I clicked it. It was a site devoted to meditation. I read on. The site discussed training the mind to induce a certain state of consciousness. It was talking about getting to a state where the mind was more open. I started to think that maybe I could use what they were teaching to train my mind to be more closed instead. All I knew was that I needed to do something to try and learn to control this thing that had taken over my life, so I gave meditation a try.

A short while later I was sitting on the floor in my room. My legs were crossed, my back was straight and my eyes were closed. My hands rested loosely on my knees and I focused on my breath as it slid past my lips. I had never tried to meditate before and at first the experience was uninspiring. I couldn't focus. My ears zoned in on the ceiling fan. It was broken and made a clicking noise, spinning and creaking like a door with a rusty hinge. Incessantly, eternally, round and round, rotating on an uneven axis; an involuntary metronome keeping the tempo of my silence in key.

I grew bored, unsure of what I was supposed to be doing, but I stuck with it. I sat still and silent and tried to relax. After some time, I did. After a while I stopped thinking about what I was doing and just let my mind go blank. I stopped focusing on the clicking of my ceiling fan and started to focus on me. It was then that I became aware of myself. I was aware of my lungs expanding like an eagle's wings preparing for flight and constricting like a snake smothering its prey. I was aware of my heart and every beat it made as if each were purposeful like the beats from the percussion section of an orchestra. I felt every part of me, even those that I had previously thought insignificant, in a new and fascinating way. I was aware of the blood flowing through my veins and the synapses between neurons in my brain. I felt composed, unified and serene. Meditating was like a drug. It made me feel euphoric and at peace.

I don't know if my experience was similar to what other people go through when they meditate, or if it was specific to me because of my ability, if maybe the openness of my mind allowed me to reach a place that other's only get a taste of in a dream. But it made me feel like I was floating on a cloud. In that moment, I felt like I could control any part of my body if I chose to. I felt like I could have slowed the blood in my veins or told my skin not to feel. I could have stopped my heart from beating just by thinking it. It was in that moment that I realized I could choose not to hear the voices. I just had to will my body not to. I simply hadn't known how to do that before, and I still wasn't sure that I knew it then, but I did know it was possible and that I could figure it out.

Ivy, I heard.

If he had thought it or said it aloud I didn't know. What I did know was that it brought me out of my meditative state. My eyes burst open and I felt like I'd come crashing down from the cloud I'd been sitting on to land ungracefully on hard cement. I suddenly felt like my bones were made of lead, and I took a deep breath to calm myself. Brant stood in my room and my eyes narrowed in on him. He stepped toward me and shut my bedroom door behind him.

"What are you doing here?" I asked him.

He held up a green spiral notebook. "Psych homework," he said and threw the notebook into my lap, "wouldn't want you to fall behind."

I stared at him skeptically.

"'Kay fine," he caved, "I was wondering how you were doing with," he held his hands up to his head and wiggled his fingers, "the thing. You weren't in class so..."

"So you were... what, worried about me?"

"*Please*, I'm... mildly interested in your... weirdness."

"Gee, thanks, but seeing as I don't care about keeping you entertained with my freak-show abilities, you can leave." I stood up then grabbing the notebook, tossing it onto my bed.

"Hey, come on now, don't be like that."

"And how should I be? The only reason you're talking to me is because you think I'm weird. Before this you were just *that guy* that got out of trouble 'cause his daddy's a big shot lawyer and screwed over one of my best friends."

His eyes narrowed, "What did Tiana tell you?"

"Does it matter?"

His lips thinned. "Look, I realize you don't think very highly of me, and I realize that's because I've... well I've given you reason not to think very highly of me. But I'm realizing that there's a lot more to you then I used to think, and I'm not just talking about the mind reading thing. You're not just some goody two shoes sheep following around Christy Noonan, you've got a mind of your own, you're willing to stand up for your friends. You're willing to leave Christy alone on a beach when she's being a pushy bitch. Yeah, I heard about that, gossip you know.

"I'm just saying. Maybe there's more to me than you used to think too."

I sighed. He looked at me with bottomless eyes that were a turbulent blue. His expression was hopeful and he pursed his lips for a moment.

"You haven't told anyone else about what you can do?"

"They wouldn't understand," I said and he nodded. "They wouldn't believe me."

"No, they wouldn't, but I do. Maybe you think I'm a dick and feel like you can't trust me, but I haven't told anyone about anything that's happened to you. That should count for something... So, it's up to you. You can kick me out but you'll be alone in this; or you can talk to me. I'm not gonna lie, yeah, I think this is strange and interesting, but at least you won't be alone."

I sighed and thought for a moment. Brant's intentions were far from noble, but he was honest. I looked at him, his eyes searching me, eyebrows just slightly downward turned and his lips drawn thin. He was waiting in anticipation. I didn't want to be dealing with this alone. I didn't want to be dealing with this at all, and Brant wasn't the person I wanted to share my thoughts with on the subject. But he was right about one thing. He was the only person I had who knew about my gift, and he didn't think I was crazy.

"Fine," I said.

He smiled a cocky grin then quickly wiped it from his face. "Right, so… how've you been?"

I shrugged. "I was peaceful until you showed up."

He looked at me confused.

"I was meditating. I'm trying to figure out how to… control it, or block it out."

"Meditating?" He looked skeptical.

"Yeah," I said in a serious tone.

He held up his hands in mock defense. "Alright, alright, did it work?"

"I don't know… I haven't had a chance to test it yet."

"Okay, so, let's test it now." He seemed excited.

"Alright, well… think something," I said with a shrug.

Um, okay. Can you hear me?

"Yep."

"Alright, well try and block me out now."

I sighed and tried to focus. I felt nervous at first, worried that I wouldn't be able to do it.

I'll just keep thinking stuff and you let me know when you can't hear me anymore.

I was trying to keep him out but his words kept flowing through my head.

And I'm guessing you can still hear me since

you're starting to look frustrated.

It was then that I realized that I was never going to block him out like that.

Come on, Ivy, you can get this.

I closed my eyes and took a deep breath. I let myself relax. I stopped focusing on what he was saying and focused on me, focused on what I wanted to do.

And I'm running out of things to think...

And then it stopped. Like an infant learning to walk, one second I was sitting, and the next I was strolling across the room. It was almost instinctive, as easy as telling my legs to walk or my lips to smile. I just... turned it off.

I opened my eyes. My lips curved up into a grin. I didn't hear him. His eyes searched mine for a moment and he could tell that I'd figured it out.

"I don't hear you anymore," I said.

"You did it," he said, seeming happy for me, but then he frowned. "What if you can't turn it back on?"

I thought for a moment about opening up my mind.

What if she's just killed her gift?

"Didn't kill it," I said and he smiled.

"Well, good, you've got it all figured out then. No more collapsing on the common."

"I don't know if I've got it down pat, but it definitely seems like a step in the right direction."

We both smiled, looking at one another. Neither of us said a word, and then the silence became awkward and we both looked away.

"Well, that's, ah, that's great. I should get going, but I'll see you around," he said and then walked out of my room closing the door behind him.

8

The Things You were Never Supposed to Hear

That night at dinner, I practiced being able to control my telepathy. I would later come to regret that decision and would wish that I had left it turned it off. Understanding what I could do was helping me to appreciate what had happened to me, but there are still times when ignorance is bliss. Some secrets you wish would have stayed secrets. Some secrets are hard on you to know.

Dad was home for dinner that night. When he walked through the door he set his briefcase down and grabbed Sadie, picking her up and swinging her around with a hug. Mom was in the dining room setting the table and the house was filled with the warm aroma of a home cooked meal.

"Hey, Kid," he said to me as I walked past.

I smiled and he followed me into the dining room.

"So, what's Mom got cooking for dinner tonight? Smells good."

"It's lasagna," Sadie said with excitement.

Dad was still carrying her. He set her down when Mom walked in with the pan of lasagna in her hands.

"Hi, honey," my mom said, setting the pan on the table and giving my father a kiss on the lips.

We all sat down to eat. I kept my mind reading abilities turned off while Mom scooped lasagna onto Sadie's plate and I waited for the spatula to be free. I was surprised at how easy it was to keep their thoughts out. It was like I had been standing in a bright room before, the lights there were so strong that I was blinded by them. They had hurt my eyes and strained my senses and then after meditating it was as if someone had led my hand to the light switch and I flipped it off. I just had to be shown where the switch was and then I knew where to find it from then on out. After discovering how to turn the lights on and off, I could do it with ease.

So I left the lights off and had a normal dinner with my family. I listened to Sadie talk about her day in Mrs. Dean's third grade class and the sound of my father's deep voice as he laughed. Sadie had been telling a story about finger painting with a boy named Billy Frank in art class which my father had found quite funny. The sound of his voice was comforting. I realized then how little I'd heard it lately. Mom smiled as well, seeming just as happy as the rest of us that he was there. She talked about a house she was trying to sell and tried to convince my dad that they should remodel the kitchen. I gave an update to my parents about school and my grades, as well as slyly snuck in a comment about the winter formal and the need to go dress shopping. All together it was a nice dinner; it made me feel connected with my family, made me feel normal.

Then my father's phone rang. I watched him pull it out of his pocket and couldn't help but hit the switch in my mind. I turned the lights on and as he looked at his phone his thoughts channeled into my head.

Liz, he thought reading the text on his phone. *I'm missing you too, babe.*

My brow creased and my lips bowed down into a frown as he slid the phone back into his pocket. I shut the light back off and it felt like a door slamming shut in my mind. My nice, normal family dinner shattered, sending shards of my broken respect raining down around me. I didn't want to hear anything else.

"Who was that?" my mom asked him.

"John from work, he needs me back there for an hour or so tonight."

Liar, I thought wanting to scream it out loud. My stomach flipped and I felt like I wanted to vomit.

"Oh really?" I could tell my mom was disappointed.

"Yeah, I'm sorry honey, I'll be back before you go to bed, promise."

He wouldn't be back before she went to sleep. I would wait up that night to see.

"Least you're home for dinner daddy," Sadie said before shoveling another fork full of saucy pasta into her mouth.

I looked at her. She was so innocent and unassuming with her bright eyes and sauce covered grin, looking at our father like he were some kind of superhero just for making it to dinner. I looked at Mom. She was disappointed but still blissfully unaware of what Dad was really leaving to do that night. And just what was he leaving to do, I wondered? He was going to see a woman named Liz, but that didn't have to mean that he was having an affair. He was just going to see a woman, a woman that he called 'babe'; a woman that he missed, that he lied about. I bit down hard on my next bite of lasagna, grinding my teeth together and trying to push the thoughts away.

I thought about never opening my mind up again after that. I thought about leaving the lights off permanently, about smashing the bulbs, or ripping out all of the wiring and living in the dark. Not that I could. Instead I was silent the rest of dinner and kept my eyes drawn down at my plate.

I went to my room after Mom had gone to bed. The small TV that sat atop my dresser was off but I spent an hour staring at it, watching the numbers turn on the digital clock of cable box.

The next day Mom drove me to school as my Scion had spent the last two nights in the student lot. On the way there, I remember looking at her as she smiled and feeling my stomach knot as if some Boy Scout were trying to earn a merit badge with my intestines. I wanted to tell her about what I'd heard

Dad think, and then at the same time I wished I'd never heard him think it in the first place. I didn't want to hurt her, but I didn't want to let her go on being hurt either. In the end I chose not to say anything. Maybe it was just because I didn't know how.

She dropped me off and I approached my friends on the courtyard. They greeted me with concerned stares. I'd disappeared early on Monday, didn't show up on Tuesday, and hadn't said a word to any of them since. Both Christy and Ti had texted me but I hadn't responded to either of them. It was no wonder they looked at me the way they did as I approached. It was as if I'd been gone for months and suddenly returned.

"She's alive," Eliza said as I approached.

"You okay?" Tiana asked.

"You sick or something?" Christy added.

"She was prob'ly just playing hooky," Damon said. "Right, Ivy?"

I laughed. "No, I think I got food poisoning or something. I'm all better now though."

"Well good," Christy said. "You won't miss any more lunch hour drama." She spoke as if she had forgiven me for leaving her on the beach the Saturday before or, more accurately, as if she had forgotten all about it.

"What drama?"

"Monday at lunch, Eric Thompson took a nose dive into the pavement," Eliza said. "Ryan Morgan tripped him and he ended up with a nose bleed."

Tiana sighed. "It wasn't *just* a nose bleed, he was gushing blood."

"Ryan Morgan, as in captain of the football team Ryan?" I knew the name instantly. Ryan was always competing for attention with Kyle Allaway the quarterback.

"Yup," Christy said. "Chase was giving me all the details about it. I guess Eric has gym with like half the football team and they've been playing all kinds of pranks on him."

"Pranks?"

"Just guy stuff," Damon said, "you know, locker room horseplay, nothing serious, just goofing around."

"Right," I said not sure what to think.

Eric was a heavyset guy with a quiet, sweet demeanor. He didn't seem like the kind of person to enjoy joking around with the football jocks. For a moment, thinking about him and his giant teddy bear like ways made me feel bad for him and the possible torture I could imagine him enduring in gym. Then another thought occurred to me. Monday had been when I took a spill out on the common on my way to lunch. It had been when I heard someone think about everyone on campus being dead a month from now. Could that have been Eric's voice I heard? He didn't seem like the kind of guy who'd want to hurt anyone, not even someone who'd hurt him. But he was being picked on and the timing was right.

The bell rang shortly after that and I went to class, keeping my gift turned off. I didn't leave the lights out for the whole day however. By lunch my curiosity got the better of me. I let the thoughts of my friends in. At first the voices all came at once. I wasn't able to filter or focus; they just came tumbling in, reverberating and resounding, echoing against the inside of my skull. I closed my eyes and lowered my head. My fingers went to rub my temples as the pain started to set in. Then, I focused on my breathing. With each long deep breath the voices thinned. Soon the hundreds that I was hearing were only ten, and then I was able to focus on just my friends before me. I smiled, glad that I had gotten control of it.

God, I would kill for Nicolette's new Prada bag. Christy was practically drooling at the brunette across the courtyard as she flaunted her new purse. *And it's not like I can get the same one, lucky bitch got it first.*

Ti pulled her hair back into a ponytail. *Field hockey practice last night was brutal.* She winced then rubbed her arm. She looked at Christy and took notice of the small salad she was eating. *Calorie counting again, she has no idea how good she has it. Girl's thin as a rail. I play two sports and all she does is starve herself for one meal and she's got a better body then me.*

I sighed. Their thoughts were petty and vain, and while I'm sure if I paid attention to my own inner dialogue I'd find more than a few self-indulgent thoughts here and there, it seemed as if the only things that Christy in particular thought about was keeping her status at the top of the social totem pole.

"You alright there, Ivy?" Tiana asked me. "You've been quiet lately."

"Yeah, I was just thinking about Eric," and I had been earlier.

"What about him?" Christy asked.

"It's just... After Ryan tripped him, did no one go to help him?"

"Mostly we all just laughed. The guy's a big tub of lard."

"He must have been so embarrassed."

Tiana sighed. "Yeah, well that's life. It's tough but it's just how it is."

I frowned at their complete lack of compassion. It would have been the right thing to help Eric up and it bothered me that neither of them even seemed to consider that. You don't always do the right thing, especially when you're seventeen, but they refused to even recognize what the right thing had been. I wondered if they'd always been this shallow and self-absorbed and I just hadn't noticed. I wondered if I was only realizing this about them after being able to hear their thoughts. Either way, in that moment I felt disappointed with them.

9

Follow Me Down

Thursday morning, Eliza convinced Christy and
Tiana to go off campus with her and Damon for
lunch. I was invited as well but didn't want to go.
They teased me, thinking I refused their invite
because I didn't want to break the rules. They didn't
know that I'd already broken my 'I've never skipped
class' streak. They said we wouldn't get caught and
not to be lame, but that wasn't why I didn't want to
go. They were gossiping about the winter formal and
again making plans to get a hotel room. They even
seemed to have convinced Tiana to go in on their
plan. I said I wouldn't be going because, in all
honesty, I wasn't in the mood for idle gossip. I didn't
feel like talking about jewelry and shoes or the way
Mallory Kinney's hips looked huge in the dress she
wore to homecoming. So when lunch came around, I
grabbed a bagel and went to the library.

The library, along with the school store, was run

by students in the DECA program on their study hall or lunch time. That day, a girl with long, dark brown hair that lightened up to blonde at the tips was working behind the checkout desk. Her hair was curled into a loose wave and floated around her face, framing her pale skin and dark lined eyes. She gave me an annoyed look when I first walked up to the counter. I had the book I wanted in one hand and my half-eaten bagel in the other. Her eyes flashed at the 'no food or drinks allowed' sign, but she said nothing. I checked out a book on telepathy and took a seat at one of the tables.

I finished my bagel before I'd even made it past the prologue, and by the time I got half way into the first chapter I was growing bored. It consisted of a lot of opinionated and vague ideas about the possibility of telepathy, none of which were really helping me with my specific and very real situation. So I pretended to continue reading and instead opened up my mind to listen in on those around me.

I saw Skyler Bishop sitting in the corner with his headphones on. His shaggy hair fell into his face and he was singing along with *The Smashing Pumpkins* in his head. He looked like he had gone out to the parking lot to get stoned and was sitting in the library to quietly live out the rest of his high. On the other side of the room, I tuned into the sound of a girl reading *The Great Gatsby.* To her right another girl was proofreading a paper, mentally chiding herself for bad punctuation, and to her left there were two rows of computers with probably six or so guys looking things up on the web. I was about to focus in on what they were looking up when he sat down before me.

"Hey," Brant said.

I looked up from my book and stared at him, annoyed. "Hey."

He snatched the telepathy book out of my hands and started to flip through it. "Doing homework?" he asked.

"Give that back."

He smirked at me. "Make me," he said and I glared at him.

"You know, you're really pushy sometimes." I eyed him with an annoyed expression.

He said something then, but I didn't hear him. The sound of his voice was a soft murmur at the back of my mind, something else was at the front.

It won't be a big enough explosion, we need more.

I tuned into the voice the same way I would if someone had just said my name. It was the same voice I'd heard on Monday, the one that had said 'a month from now they'll all be dead.' I still didn't know who the voice belonged to, but it was one I'd never forget. The deep and rough tone of his speech sounded pained in my mind, pained and angry.

"Hey, are you listening to me?" Brant asked.

I ignored him and abruptly stood up. My telepathy book sat forgotten on the table.

It's gotta take out the whole school, I don't want anyone to survive.

My head jerked to look around the room as his

words sent a wave of panic through me. Frantically, my eyes scanned the library looking from face to face, but I didn't know where the voice had come from and there was so much of the library I couldn't see. I walked toward the rows of computers where all I could see were the tops of students' heads. I listened for him, but I didn't hear him think anything else. Spinning around I saw the stacks on the other side of the room where students could be standing between the rows of books, out of view. I twisted my head around looking and listening until the room was a spiraling blur, but nothing else came to me.

Brant put his hand on my shoulder and stopped me from my panicked rotation. He looked at me with concerned eyes. I ran a hand through my hair, pulling at the amber stands. I didn't know what to do or even what to think. Someone was planning to blow up the school.

"Ivy, what's wrong?" Brant asked with true concern. "What did you hear?"

My mouth fell open but no words came out. I couldn't speak, and then the bell rang and I watched as all the students in the library got up gathering their things and began to walk out. The nausea I felt was as if all of my organs had detached and were rearranging themselves inside my body. What I had heard frightened me and I begin to tremble. My breath came out in short, shaky pants and my eyes flickered frantically around the room. Brant was still looking at me expectantly but I couldn't talk to him, so I ran. I rushed out through the library doors and started to weave past students in the hallway.

I raced to my next class trying to distance myself from the library where the words of whatever twisted individual that wanted to kill us all still rang through my mind. I was also running from Brant. I didn't want to tell him what I'd heard. It would make it all too real. I knew things I wasn't supposed to know and I didn't know how to deal with that. So I tried to escape the responsibility that was running me down, chasing me like a wolf on the tail of a rabbit. The only problem was my next class was Psychology and I wouldn't be able to escape Brant for long.

I turned off my gift. I blocked out the voices. I didn't want to hear what Brant was thinking. He sat down at his desk a short while after I did and glared at me. I refused to look at him. I heard him sigh and could tell by the way he clenched his jaw and rolled his eyes up to the ceiling that he was frustrated with me. Mrs. Rochester arrived and started her lecture, continuing on with Freud. I tried to pay attention to her but soon realized that Brant hadn't given up on trying to talk to me.

Ivy! I heard in my head.

I visibly flinched. Despite my efforts to block out all voices, he had broken through and my name rang in my head loudly as if he'd yelled in my ear. I turned toward him with a glare that was razor sharp. He smirked.

'Stop it,' I mouthed.

We need to talk after class.

'Fine,' I rolled my eyes and went back to focusing on Mrs. Rochester's lecture. To my right I could see Brant gloating in silence as he leaned back in his chair with a grin on his face.

After class Brant practically cornered me in the hallway. He followed me out of class and walked with me down the hall until he could pull me off to the side by the lockers where we were out of the way of foot traffic. He glared down at me expectantly waiting for me to talk.

"Well, what happened back there? You went all like *The Shining* on me in the library."

"I heard something."

Behind me a noisy group of guys moved down the hallway and distracted me. I looked in their direction as they walked past and I realized that I still didn't know who this person was that wanted to kill us all. He could be anyone.

"I... can we talk later, when we're not... *here*?"

Brant looked around. He grabbed me by the arm then and pulled me down the hall.

"Come on, Daniels."

"What, where are we going?"

"Somewhere not *here*."

"We can't just..."

Brant stopped walking. "What? Leave? Don't tell me you've never ditched before, I've seen you."

I remembered the day I first started hearing the voices and how when I left I'd walked past Brant in the parking lot.

"Fine," I said jerking my arm free and followed

him out of the school.

We made our way to the student lot, both of us keeping our eyes open for the school security guard or Mrs. Farrow. Luckily neither was in sight. I followed Brant to his car and got in the passenger seat. He sat down in the driver seat and I was surprised when he started the car.

"We don't really need to go anywhere, this is far enough."

"If I'm gonna leave school to hear what you have to say, I'm going farther than the parking lot."

He backed up and made his way out of the student lot. I sat silently for a moment, tracing the Z28 insignia on the dash. The inside of Brant's car was falling apart. The carpets were dingy, the tan leather worn. I wondered for a moment why he drove what most assuredly must be a gas guzzling tank. With his dad being well off enough to make donations to the school large enough to build a new swimming pool, I had expected him to have something... newer. He probably could've gotten a brand new Camaro if he wanted and yet he drove this.

"Why do you drive this anyway?" I asked when the curiosity finally got to be too much for me to handle.

"You don't like the Z28? She's a classic."

"Please, this car looks like it's from 1980. It's not a classic."

"1981 for your information."

"Whatever," I said, rolling my eyes, realizing that I didn't really care about the car he drove. I looked out the window for a little while. We entered one of the more wealthy subdivisions in the area, Laurel Hill Estates. I don't know if I'd really call the houses that were there 'estates' but the name made it sound fancy and I always assumed that was the point. It was the kind of place where they set rules and regulations for everything from the color you painted your house to the amount of cars you were allowed to have in the driveway at one time. Christy lived at the far end of it, but other than that I didn't really know the location.

"So, start talking," Brant said, diverting my attention from the window to look at him. "What'd you hear?"

I took a deep breath and found my nerves trembling again. "Remember when I fell on Monday?"

"Yeah?"

"Before I passed out I heard… I heard this deep voice. It said that a month from now we'd all be dead."

Brant looked to me then with a disturbed face. His eyebrows dropped low and puckered. It was then that I also realized that we'd stopped driving.

Brant sighed, "Come on, you can tell me more inside." I looked out the window at the large brick house and when I looked back to Brant, he'd already gotten out of the car so I got out.

"Where are we?" I asked shutting my car door.

"My house."

I don't know why I was surprised that he lived in such a big house, such a nice house. I knew that his father made a lot of money, I had just been thinking about it in the car, but Brant didn't seem like he belonged here. I followed him around the house to the back sliding glass door. It was unlocked and he slid it open, stepping inside without a second thought. I was hesitant about following him at first. I peered into the house. Brant was standing in the kitchen. He turned around and saw that I wasn't behind him.

"Well, come on," he said and I did.

I stepped into the kitchen and closed the sliding glass door behind me. It was a big kitchen with stainless steel appliances, dark granite counter tops, and a beautiful mosaic tile backsplash. My mom would kill to cook here, I thought.

"This way," Brant said and I saw him standing near an open door.

The door led to the basement. I followed him down and the stairs creaked as we moved. When we reached the bottom, I saw that the basement had been finished. The walls were painted a dark blue. There was no carpet, just a cold cement floor, but a large black rug took up a good amount of the space. On the wall hung a decent size flat screen TV. Below it was a short white dresser and across from it was a worn black leather sofa and small wooden coffee table. On the far wall was a queen size bed with white sheets and a blue comforter that was half-crumpled on the floor. There was no headboard but various posters from rock and heavy metal music groups lined the walls. The clothes hamper on the far wall was full, but other than that the space was relatively clean. Brant walked over to the black leather sofa and plopped down. He sat leaning back with his limbs spread out. I chose not to sit next to him and instead hovered just before the TV.

"So you heard someone say he wants us all dead in a month on Monday, what'd you hear in the library then?"

"I heard the same voice. This time... it sounded like he was looking up how to make a bomb or something. He said that it wouldn't be a big enough explosion, said it needed to be big enough that no one survived."

Brant sat up straighter, his eyes locked on me with a look of unease.

"I don't know who it was, I tried to look around to see if I could figure it out but... whoever they were they sounded serious."

"We've got to figure out who it is then."

"What?"

"Well, we know this is going to happen in about a month, we've got to stop it."

"Brant, how? The most I know about this guy is just that. He's a guy, that's all I know."

"Well, that's something, and we know that he was in the library today."

"I just... this is too much, it's too big. How am I supposed to stop it? This guy wants us all dead. He hates everyone at Alta Ladera and he's obviously really serious and... I'm just me." I thought then about what I'd do if I didn't stop it. What was my plan? Try and skip school that day and hope for the best? I couldn't just do that.

"Well we've got to try right? People are going to die otherwise, Ivy."

I knew he was right. It was the right thing to do even if I didn't think I could possibly stop it. I had to try. "Why do you care? It's not like you like anyone in our school anyway?"

I saw him stiffen. He seemed almost mad that I was questioning his motives.

"I may not like any of them, but that doesn't mean I want them all dead. Look, we know something here, and maybe we can't stop it, but we're the only ones that even have a chance to. I can't just not do anything."

I nodded, "Okay so, where do we start?" I took a step toward him and sat down at the opposite end of the sofa.

"Gotta figure out who it is first, the way I see it."

I nodded. "Then what?"

He was about to answer when we both heard a noise and I turned toward the stairs. They creaked as someone moved down them. I heard voices and then after a moment I saw Skyler and Jason emerge from the stairwell. They saw me and I watched their eyes go wide.

Brant's got a girly over, Oo lala, Jason thought as he and Skyler glanced at one another before setting their sights on Brant.

Great timing, guys, Brant thought and as he stood up, I followed suit.

"Hey Brant, you ah, ditched out without us,"

Jason said.

"Yeah and I see why," Skyler added looking at me.

"Yeah, sorry, guys. Ivy and I got partnered up in Psych for a project. We were just going over some notes. I wasn't really expecting you to stop by."

I was a little amazed at how quickly and smoothly he'd come up with the lie. For a moment I wondered if we really did have a Psych project that we were supposed to be working on.

"Yeah I bet you weren't." Jason jabbed Skyler in the ribs.

"Right, well I'm gonna go take Ivy home and I'll be back here in a few."

"I'll, um, I'll be in the car," I said and walked up the stairs.

Brant lingered in the basement as I walked up the stairs. Before I even reached the top step, I heard his friends questioning him about me. I walked to the top of the stairs then stopped to listen. For a moment I felt guilty about being nosy, but then I realized that I could listen in on people's private thoughts and that made me not feel so bad about eavesdropping.

"You've got a thing for the Daniels girl," Jason said and I could picture Brant glancing at the stairs as if to assure himself that I'd gone up them.

"I saw you and her in the library together today," Skyler added.

"I don't have a thing for Ivy. She's just my partner on this Psych thing... that's all."

For some reason when he said that, it hurt a

little.

"Sure thing, man."

"Seriously, guys, the only Daniels I like is Jack... which you better have brought over by the way."

"Of course," Jason said. I pictured him pulling the square bottle out of his bag.

"Well good then, lemme go take this chick home and then we can have ourselves some fun."

I heard him start to walk up the stairs and I quickly moved away from the door.

"Just don't start drinking 'til I get back," he called down to them.

By then I was on the other side of the kitchen standing before the sliding glass door.

"Ready to go?" he asked me.

"Yup," I replied.

I was silent when we got into the car and he looked at me but said nothing. As we drove, I noticed that he'd shoot me a glance every few minutes, but the ride continued to be quiet until I realized that we weren't on our way back to school, back to my car. We were driving toward my house.

"Hey, wait you have to take me to my car," I said.

"I'm already half-way to your house."

"I can't get to school tomorrow without my car."

He gave a frustrated sigh. "I'll pick you up tomorrow, 'kay?"

My lips thinned. "Fine, whatever," I said.

"Are you mad at me or something?"

Was I? I didn't know. It wasn't like he did anything for me to be mad at him for. Hell, he'd offered to help me figure out who wanted to blow up the entire school. Still though, I felt upset with him.

"No, I'm not mad," I said and tried to forget the strange little twist that I'd felt in my stomach.

10

I was Hoping You were Different

Brant arrived at my house the next morning earlier than I expected. I opened the car door and saw him sitting there leaning back in his seat, one hand on the wheel, and his seatbelt, unbuckled, hanging loose by the door. It smelled like smoke, which both Brant and his car always did, but more so just then, as if he'd just tossed his cigarette out the window before pulling up to my house. I got in and we took off in the direction of school with more speed than necessary. I quickly buckled my seatbelt. He turned to me after a moment and looked me up and down.

"So, I've got an idea on where we should start to look for our mystery murderer."

"Alright, what've you got?" I asked glad that he had an idea of where to start, as I was still feeling like all of this was out of my league.

"Craig Fister."

"Huh?"

"Craig Fister."

"Not a clue."

"He's in my Physics class, my grade, dreadlocks, 'hates the world' attitude, one of those totally self-absorbed types that thinks he's the only person on the face of the planet to ever have anything bad happen to him. I heard he skinned a cat last year for kicks and giggles. Seems like our type."

I nodded. I didn't really know who Craig was, but off Brant's description he definitely seemed like someone we should check out. I had someone else in mind that I wanted to talk to though, someone who didn't seem as obviously homicidal as Craig.

"I wanna talk to Eric Thompson too." I said.

"Teddy Bear Thompson, the guy looks big enough to crush the whole school with his gut, but he doesn't seem like the type to go all *Unabomber.*"

"Ryan Morgan gave him a nosebleed at lunch on Monday. Guess some of the football players in his gym class have been giving him a hard time too."

"You're thinking he might be out for revenge?"

"I'm thinking that maybe he's getting sick of being picked on."

Brant nodded. We were silent the rest of the short ride to school. The air whistled through my window, as it was open only a crack, but I didn't roll it up. Without the radio, I had nothing but that shrill to occupy my thoughts and I focused on it to keep from thinking about Eric. Even still, my mind conjured the image of *Teddy Bear* Thompson filling a pipe bomb and lighting its fuse. Brant was right, that image didn't look right. Eric was a warm, good natured person. He didn't have a lot of friends but he was nice to everyone. He didn't seem like the kind of person to try and blow up the school. Still, I was learning that people weren't always how they appeared to be. Brant pulled into the student lot and turned off the car. We sat there for a moment then he turned to me.

Sorry for my friends being dicks the other day, he thought and I rolled my eyes. He wanted to apologize but couldn't even say it aloud. Then I saw his jaw twitch just ever so slightly and realized that this wasn't easy for him to do.

"Don't worry about it," I said and we exited the car.

As I shut the door, I looked up and caught sight of something a row over from where Brant and I were standing. Tiana looked on at me with disgust. I didn't even have a chance to say her name, to wave, to think anything as she stormed off away from me.

How could she? I heard her think as she stomped through the parking lot. For a moment all I could do was watch her go.

Shit, I heard Brant think then.

I glanced back at him for a moment and then chased after my friend. Ti had made it all the way to the courtyard before I caught up to her. I had been calling her name as I chased after her but she didn't stop. She didn't turn around. She was pissed at me. Finally her feet reached the grass and she slowed to a stop. She took a deep breath and then spun around to face me. Her eyes were pointed and fiery with anger, her fists clenching at her sides. I was still trying to catch my breath.

You are such a bitch, I heard her think.

"Ti."

"What were you doing with Brant, Ivy?"

"Nothing."

"Nothing? He drove you to school, and I saw you two talking the other day, what the hell is that about?" *I really liked him and he hurt me.*

"We… we were just…" my mind raced for an excuse. "We got partnered up in Psych for this project, that's all." I figured if I was going to lie that I might as well keep to the same one.

"So what, you were up working on this project at like six a.m. or something? He drove you to school, Ivy. What the hell? I told you he's an asshole, that… look, I just don't get why you're hanging out with him… I don't get it at all."

She spun away from me again and stormed off. I watched her go. Tiana made her way to where Christy and Eliza were talking. Damon was nowhere in sight. I saw her say something to the other girls, and the way their expressions changed to shock and disgust. The three of them stood there looking down on me as if they were the *Weird Sisters* straight out of *Macbeth*, deciding my fate and predicting my demise.

Ivy's really been falling off the deep end lately, Christy thought.

What is she thinking, hanging out with a loser like Brant? That was Eliza. *She's got it so good, why would she want to be around him?*

I didn't approach them. I just stood where I was and looked on. I felt terrible, felt like I'd betrayed Tiana, and like she'd betrayed me. She was over there now, most certainly telling them about how she'd seen me hanging out with Brant and what a lowlife he was, but I'm sure she left out the part where she hooked up with him at Nicolette's party. There's no way she'd admit to having a crush on the school bad boy, not to the Queen C, Christy Noonan. No, they wouldn't understand that she'd had feelings for him. If they knew that, they'd have been looking at her the way they were looking at me, appalled. Ti wasn't really disgusted with me for hanging out with Brant, not unless she was disgusted with herself for it too. No, she was hurt. She felt like I'd swooped in and gone after a guy that she wasn't over yet and that wasn't okay with her.

What hurt the most was that I wasn't even doing anything wrong. I didn't steal her crush away from her, maybe she still wanted Brant but I didn't. I didn't want him at all. We weren't even really friends, least not voluntary ones. Brant and I were hanging out by circumstance and nothing more, but I couldn't explain any of that to them.

"I'm sorry," I heard Brant say as he walked up behind me. He put his hand on my shoulder but I shook it off.

"Don't" I said with resentment in my voice. "Just stay away from me," and I walked off.

I had my Monday/Wednesday classes that Friday, which meant I had first hour with Tiara. I walked into the math room and saw that she had taken a seat on the far side of the room. She glanced at me as I entered then turned her head.

She better not even try to sit by me, she thought.

So I sat on the other side of the room in a seat as close to the door as I could manage. I tried not to listen to her thoughts as Math went on but found I couldn't help myself.

She was the only one I trusted to tell her that I'd been seeing Brant and then she betrays me.

I felt a stab of guilt but I also picked up on something else. She'd just thought that she'd been seeing Brant. She only told me she'd hooked up with him and just what that meant exactly she hadn't clarified. I realized then that she hadn't told me the entire story, and to some degree that made me feel worse.

Guess I can really stop hoping that we'll get back together now.

I tried to talk to her after the bell rang, tried to apologize, but she walked past and refused to even acknowledge me. After that my mind was a daze through both Lit and Bio as my entire body sat fuming with rage. I couldn't think about anything but what had transpired that morning and it all made me so angry. I was angry that Tiana hadn't told me the whole story about her and Brant, angry that Brant had hurt her, angry that I had hurt her. I was mad that I had told Brant about the things that have been going on with me and hadn't told my friends, mad that I felt like I couldn't tell them, and I was mad at the fact that this had happened to me to begin with.

All of it made me want to explode, made me want to scream, but I felt like there was nothing I could do about it. Tiana wasn't talking to me. I couldn't get rid of Brant as he was the only one who knew about my ability, as well as possibly the only person willing to talk to me at all at the moment. I couldn't dispose of my ability and on top of it I still had to somehow stop the school from getting blown up.

By the time I walked out of Bio, my nerves were a knotted ball. I felt like a compressed coil ready to spring. So when Brant grabbed me by the arm and yanked me down an empty hallway, I had to curb the instinct to punch him straight in the nose.

"I don't want to talk to you right now," I said.

"Yeah, well, you're gonna listen."

"I don't care what you have to say. Tiana…"

"Tiana what? Told you that I'm a dick? That I got some then got gone, yeah? That I won't talk to her anymore?"

I didn't nod, I just glared at him.

"Did she tell you *why* I won't talk to her anymore?" *No probably not,* he thought. "Well *I'll* tell you… Tiana and I were seeing each other, for almost a month."

"What?"

"Yeah, she left that part out, huh?" Brant looked around. The halls were filled with students as they met with friends before lunch, stopped in classrooms to talk to teachers or went to grab things from their lockers. "Come on, let's talk somewhere else."

I followed him out. We avoided the common and walked out a side door. I kept my arms crossed as we moved, still not fully ready to trust or believe him. We stepped outside and Brant dug his hands into his pockets searching for something. Then after a moment he pulled out a pack of cigarettes, Marlboro Reds, and tugged one out of the box. He had a cheap plastic blue lighter that'd been stuffed in the pack among his smokes. He pulled it out as well and lit up. I watched as he inhaled, the end of his cigarette glowing orange.

I thought Tiana was different. He exhaled and ribbons of white smoke spiraled up into the sky.

"So talk, that's what we're out here for isn't it."

He took another drag of his cigarette. "A few weekends ago, there was that big house party on Longview Drive."

"Nicolette's house, yeah, I was there. Ti said you and her hooked up that night."

"Hooked up? We made out in some bedroom on the second floor, wasn't much more than that and it certainly wasn't the first time... I had shown up that night because she said she'd be there. We were seeing each other on the down low, didn't really want to make a big deal out of it. At least, that's what I thought it was about. Turns out Tiana just didn't want to tell her friends about me.

"God forbid she date someone who isn't a jock or on the honor role. That night she walked in with

Christy, I was in the living room talking with Jason by the keg. I waved at Tiana and she took one glance back at Christy and turned away." He took another drag of his cigarette and looked up squinting into the sun. "It wasn't until after Christy disappeared with two brainless lugs that Tiana said a single word to me. I wanted to know what was going on. If she was serious about me, and I thought she was, then she shouldn't be ashamed to be seen with me. So I asked her about it. She gave me some bullshit about not seeing me when she walked in and when I said that maybe we should start doing more things together, maybe meet each other's friends, she got pissed at me and asked me why I was trying to ruin what we had.

"The truth of it is I didn't fit into the perfect little world her life revolved around. We met a few months ago at some beach bonfire for the field hockey team. Skyler, Jason and I were crashing it. Tiana got frustrated with one of her teammates and stormed off down the beach. I followed her, I thought she enjoyed my company cause we started to meet up every here and there after that, then we started to see one another regularly for about a month before that party. She didn't care about me though. She just used me to make herself feel better 'cause when she hung out with me I didn't ask anything of her like everyone else does. But it doesn't matter. It was never about me, just the escape I offered her.

He took a deep breath. "I figured it out that night at that house party. So yeah, I said screw it and had one more good night fooling around with her in

Nicolette's or whoever's house that was, and I told her I was done with it and I left."

I was silent for a moment. I didn't know what to say. He looked genuinely hurt by what had happened between him and Tiana and his story did seem to fit with what I knew. Tiana had always been a good friend though. I didn't want to think that she was as selfish as she seemed to be, but after having heard her thoughts I began to realize that Brant's version of the events made perfect sense. Christy was extremely judgmental, and I had always known that about her, but it was even more apparent after being able to hear her thoughts. We were all so concerned with what other people thought about us, with what she had thought about us, that it didn't surprise me that Tiana had kept her relationship hidden from us. There was pressure being a girl at Alta Ladera High, pressure to be liked, to be considered pretty and smart and athletic. You wanted to live up to what everyone thought you should be, what your parents, teachers, coaches, girlfriends, cute boys all thought you should be.

Christy would have looked down on Tiana for seeing Brant. She would have been mean and I can understand how that would have been scary for Ti. But it wasn't right. Tiana couldn't stand up to Christy or any of us when it came to her and Brant, and she had sold me out to their judgmental critiques.

"I'm sorry, I didn't know." I finally said. He nodded.

"I just hope you're different, don't know why I'm letting you in to all of this because I thought she was different too. But that day you thought I called her a bitch, thought I called you one too, and you got right in my face about it and stood up for what you thought was right." *None of those other girls woulda done that for you.*

I winced at his thought, but he was right. Even now they were all off sitting at our usual lunch table and they were talking about me. I didn't have to listen in on what they were saying, didn't have to try and read their minds. I knew what they were doing, and it wasn't standing up for me. I looked at Brant, my eyes meeting his, and in that moment I felt different. Maybe it was what had happened to me that made me that way, maybe not. For whatever reason, in that moment, looking into Brant's eyes, I knew that I wasn't some petty, vain Valley girl, even if that was the kind of girl I had chosen to be friends with in the past.

"You're right," I said.

For a moment his eyes widened as if he hadn't expected me to agree with him. He looked as if he was about to say something, but then his eyes shifted. His gaze moved to focus on something behind me.

"Look," he said.

I turned around

"Eric Thompson."

I saw him then. He was walking toward the school from the student lot. He stomped as he moved, each step heavy. His black backpack was swung over one shoulder. I watched as he wiped his nose with the sleeve of his dark sweatshirt. Then I saw Brant walk past me.

"Wait, Brant, what are you doing?"

He stopped and turned back to face me. "You said you wanted to talk to him." Then he turned back around and continued walking toward Eric.

I sighed then followed after him watching as he flicked his cigarette off into the distance. Orange specks hit the asphalt and bounced back up into the air like the world's smallest fireworks.

"Hey, Eric," he called out and I watched Eric stop and turn to face us.

I caught up to Brant by the time he reached him.

"Hey," Eric said, his brown eyes bouncing back and forth between Brant and me.

"We just wanted to ask you a few things."

Eric pushed his black hair out of his eyes.

Well go on then, read his thoughts. Brant looked to me.

"It's not that easy," I mumbled. I couldn't just look at him and see if he was the person planning to kill us all. He had to think something about it that I could hear. I looked to the heavyset guy before us. "Hey, Eric, I um… I was just wondering how you're doing."

His eyes narrowed on me.

"You know, cause of, um…" I stumbled over my words unsure of what to say to him. I didn't really know him; I hadn't ever had a conversation with him.

"She heard about you taking a hit to the pavement on Monday and felt bad," Brant said.

Why do you care? I heard Eric think. "I'm doing fine."

I tried to listen closely to his voice, tried to determine if it was the same voice I heard on Monday and the day before in the library. I didn't think it was, but I couldn't tell for sure. His voice was deep, but it didn't sound quite right.

"Right, I know this is weird," I said, "I know we don't really know each other very well, I just..." then finally it came to me what to say, "I was in the library yesterday, and I saw you... you seemed, upset and..."

"Couldn't have been me," he said cutting me off. "I wasn't here yesterday... I had a dentist appointment."

"Oh, sorry then, my mistake."

An awkward moment of silence passed and after that he turned from us and continued to walk toward the school.

Really weird.

Brant turned to me. "So, that's it, we're sure it's not him?"

"He didn't sound the same, and he wasn't here yesterday, so he couldn't have been who I heard in the library."

"So why are you still staring at him as he walks away?"

I turned to face him. "He just gave me a weird vibe."

11

Keeping to Myself

The rest of Friday I spent by myself. Brant went off with Jason and Skyler so I went to the library alone. This time I checked out a collection of short stories by *Stephen King* and took note that the girl behind the counter was named Charlotte Olsen. She was reading Orwell's *1984* and used her time card as a bookmark. I didn't talk to her, but filed her name away in my memory anyway.

That night, Dad wasn't home for dinner, and I remember Mom being quieter than usual. I chose not to listen in on what she was thinking. I didn't want to know what was bothering her. After we ate, I helped Sadie with her math homework then pulled out the checkers board that dad and I used to play with when I was Sadie's age. I let her win a few games.

That weekend, I stayed in. It had been months since I'd spent a weekend at home. Months since I'd chosen to hang out with my mom and watch a movie instead of going out to a party, on a date or out to the mall with friends. Saturday night, when Mom and I were watching some romanticized vampire film and ate microwave popcorn, I realized that I'd missed doing that. I missed lounging on the sofa in my sweats with my hair pulled up in a pony, missed talking with my mom and laughing through mouthfuls of buttery popcorn goodness. It felt refreshing to have a night being me again, to have a night where I didn't have to care about what to wear or if I'd say the wrong thing or if I was wearing enough makeup, or too much. It was fun, hanging out with Mom and Sadie. It made me feel normal again.

I didn't talk to Tiana or Christy at all that weekend, didn't call Eliza to see what they'd been saying about me. I simply didn't care. They could say what they wanted. For once I simply didn't give a shit what they thought of me.

On Sunday, I woke up early feeling great. Mom made blueberry pancakes for breakfast along with homemade grapefruit juice, and we all sat together to eat at the table. I watched as Sadie slathered syrup over her cakes then watched as Dad came down the stairs dressed for work.

"Emily, have you seen my blue tie?" He held a dark red tie in his hand and looked at my mother expectantly.

I saw him smile at me from where I was sitting at the kitchen table. Mom walked up to him then and gave him a peck on the lips.

"It's at the drycleaners." She took the red tie he

held and wrapped it around his neck. "This one will look just fine."

Dad tilted his head as she secured the knot. "Yeah, that's what I thought."

"I can't believe they're making you go in on a Sunday," Mom said. Her fingers were fidgeting with the lapels of his suit coat.

"I know I've been at the office a lot lately, but I'll only be gone a few hours today. I promise." Dad looked over to Sadie and me. "Love you girls, I'll see you tonight," he said and Sadie waved.

I didn't wave or say goodbye. I was listening to his thoughts.

God, it's already gotten so late. He was looking at his watch. *Liz was expecting me ten minutes ago. If I didn't have to get all dressed up like I was going to work, this would be so much easier.* "Well I've got to go, I'm already late."

"Have a good day, honey."

He waved once more and then he was out the door.

12

Sorry Charlie

Brant wasn't at school on Monday. When I got there, I found myself looking around for him, but he wasn't on the common. I noticed Skyler and Jason hovering in their usual spot against the building, standing in its shadow between the parking lot and the courtyard, but they were alone. In the distance I heard laughing and murmured conversation. Students were shuffling in and meeting up on the courtyard, but there was no one I was looking for anymore. In that moment I felt alone, but it was brief.

Intervention time, I heard in Eliza's voice.

I looked across the common to see her and Christy headed my way. In the distance, Damon and Tiana sat near the fountain. They glanced at me with wary eyes.

"Ivy," Christy said as they approached. "I'm so glad to see you." Christy walked over to one side of me and Eliza went to the other. She put her arm around me and, as they flanked me, we all began to walk. "I know you've been on this sad downward spiral thing lately, but we want you to know we're here to help."

Eliza nodded in agreement. "Everyone has their moments when they're not thinking straight."

"Right, exactly, and just because you've totally lost touch with reality and have probably been hooking up with the school lost cause doesn't mean there isn't hope. We just have to look at the bright side, like how even on a diet you can still have chocolate cake. As long as it's only a little slice, you know. The point is we're here for you."

I stopped walking, forcing them to stop with me. "Alright, stop," I said. "First off, I am not and have not I been *hooking up* with the school 'lost cause,' and, second, I'm not in a downward spiral, I haven't lost it."

God, it's so much worse than I thought, "I know you're upset about Steve not being into you, but..."

"Whoa, Steve wasn't not into me, I wasn't into him. Remember, I was the one that left the beach that night. Look, I don't need your help because there's nothing wrong with me." I pushed away from them and started to walk off.

Wow, what a stuck up bitch, I heard Eliza think, but I ignored it.

"Did that really just happen?" Christy asked Eliza astonished.

Their voices faded away into the distance as I made my way inside the building.

I didn't talk to any of them again that day. I planned to spend my lunch hour in the library again and enjoy my peace and quiet. Walking through the halls on my way to the library, bagel and cream cheese in hand, I wondered where Brant was. I knew I probably shouldn't. After all, he wasn't exactly known for having great attendance, but ever since I found myself with this ability he'd been around. Most likely he was just skipping class, but I couldn't help but wonder if he were home sick or had some kind of doctor's appointment.

I sat down at a table in the library and pulled out the *Stephen King* book that I'd checked out the week before. I didn't open it though. I was thinking about the voice I'd heard in the library the week before. I was trying to think of what I should do next, what else could I do to stop the school from exploding, which in and of itself didn't sound so bad. It was the part where whoever this guy was wanted to blow it up with everyone still inside that I found disturbing.

I'd already talked to Eric Thompson and ruled him out. Brant had wanted to talk to Craig Fister, but I didn't really know who he was so I decided to wait on questioning him until Brant was back at school. Still though, there had to be something else I could do. If it wasn't Craig that I heard then we couldn't just keep talking to people one after another. There had to be a better way to narrow it down. I just didn't know how to go about trying to find someone solely on the sound of their voice.

I finished my bagel and tossed the empty cream cheese container in a nearby trash can then I picked up my book. I flipped it open to where I'd bookmarked my page and tried to let the story suck me in. But I couldn't concentrate. Every time I'd read a sentence, I'd find my mind wandering to thoughts of who this person was that wanted to kill us all. I thought about how lonely he must feel if there wasn't a single person in the entire school that he wouldn't want to see dead. I thought then about my *friends* out on the courtyard today, thought about how, for as long as I've known them, they've pushed their ideas of who I should be onto me. I thought about all the times I'd gone to a party that I didn't really want to go to because it was the place to be, or changed how I dressed or did my hair a certain way because it was in style. Sure, sometimes I did things because I liked them, but more often than not it was about fitting in, something that whoever wanted to blow up the school must have felt like they didn't do. Then I thought about Brant.

Brant didn't care what anyone thought of him. He was different from most everyone else at school, not that he wasn't judgmental. After all, he thought I was just like Christy Noonan once upon a time. But he was willing to get to know me, something I knew my friends wouldn't be willing to do for him. He was willing to keep my secret, willing to help me, to catch me when I fell.

I shook the thoughts of Brant out of my head. I

needed to focus on something else. I needed to figure out how to narrow down my search for this bomber from every male student in the school to something more manageable, like limiting it to just the people in the library last Thursday. If only I could watch the film from the school security cameras and see who had been in the library at the same time as me. I knew I couldn't do that though. Then I realized that there was one person who I could ask that might remember who'd been here a little better than me-the girl working at the front desk, Charlotte.

I got up from the table and walked over to the front desk. Charlotte was pulling her hair back into a ponytail. The light tips of it swayed as she looped the band one last time around her hair.

"Can I help you?" she asked.

"Um, yeah you can actually... this is going to seem a little odd, but you were working last Thursday when I was in here. I'm trying to find someone, a guy, that I heard talking. I don't know his name, but he was... a little off. I guess I'm just wondering if you remember anything weird from Thursday, if anyone stood out?"

She gave me a blank stare. *Anything weird? This is the library, people have some interesting ideas of what a good read is, but nothing ever happens here,* "No, I don't remember anyone standing out last Thursday." *Except maybe, you, right at the end of the hour.*

"Right, um, do you remember any of the guys who were here last Thursday?"

Other than Brant who was making googly eyes at you or his stoner friend? "Uh, a couple of guys from the football team were using the computers. I don't really pay that much attention to people. I just scan the books you know. Oh, but that creepy senior guy, the one with the dreadlocks, he was here. I heard he skinned a cat once. That guy really creeps me out." *Not to mention how screwed up is it that he gets off killing animals.*

Craig Fister, I felt like yelling out 'bingo' after she described him. "That helps a lot actually, that might have been him. Thanks, Charlotte."

"Oh, uh. It's Charlie. I go by Charlie, and you're welcome." She smiled.

I nodded then walked away. It seemed that Brant had the right idea all along. I felt relieved to possibly know who the future bomber was, but also nervous for the same reason. If it was Craig, I still didn't know how I was going to stop him.

13.

Can You find Me?

On Tuesday, I got to school earlier than I had intended, avoiding Christy and the rest of my friends, if they were still friends. At that point I wasn't sure what to consider them. I sat down in the soft grass with my book, resting my back against a tree. I didn't hear him when he approached me, not his voice nor his thoughts, but I felt him standing before me. He had a heavy presence. He could be sly enough to walk up to me without making a sound, but the second he set his eyes on me, the weight of his gaze let me know he was there. I lowered my book and looked up to see Brant. His hands were shoved deep into the pockets of his jacket; his eyes diverting their gaze as if I hadn't already know he'd been staring at me.

"Where have you been?" I asked him.

"Not here, what's it to you?"

"Someone's cranky," I said as I closed my book and stood up to face him.

He sighed. "Sorry, just haven't had a great day so far is all." He ran a hand through his hair.

"Sorry," I said.

A moment of silence passed between us.

"So, what'd I miss yesterday?"

I sighed, "Quite a bit actually. Christy and her fellow lemmings decided that I needed an intervention, so they confronted me and tried to knock some sense into me."

Brant looked to me with an expression that said he was worried they'd gotten through to me, as if anything they had said had been logical. But, he kept his cool. "How'd that go?" He asked.

"Fine. I told them to back off and that I wasn't crazy, haven't talked to any of them since. So life is good on that front."

He raised one eyebrow at me. "You're not upset about your friends not talking to you?"

"I think I'm just feeling like I need a little break from them… but that's not the most interesting thing about yesterday. I was in the library and talked to that girl at the front desk. She said Craig Fister was in the library last Thursday."

His eyes lit up. "Guess we need to have a talk with Craig then."

"That's what I'm thinking."

"And it looks like now might be our best chance to do so."

I turned around and looked to where Brant's sight was locked. Stepping off campus and walking toward the row of trees that led into a small wood on the

other side of the parking lot was who I assumed was
Craig Fister. He was tall and lanky, wearing a t-shirt
that looked too big for his frame and jeans that
sagged loose on his hips. His hair was a knotted mess
of light brown dreadlocks which lumped down around
his shoulders and his eyes moved in a shifty motion
as he kept lookout for anyone who might catch him
ditching out.

Brant didn't have to say anything to me to get me
to follow him. We both left school, listening as the
first hour bell sounded behind us. We made our way
quickly across the parking lot. The entire way, I was
hoping that this would turn out to be our guy. So far
all the signs were pointing to him. He'd been in the
right places at the right times and he had a history
that suggested he was capable of doing something so
monstrous as to try and kill us all. I realized then
that I was also a little fearful. I felt nauseous and
shaky at the thought that this was the person who
was plotting all of our deaths and wondered if it was
the wisest thing to be following him into the secluded
woods.

Despite my nerves, Brant and I went after him
anyway and I found myself swallowing to keep down
the bile that was rising in my throat. There was a
thin path that twisted through the trees and we
followed it down to a small opening where there was
a fallen tree. Craig was sitting on the fallen trunk.
His gaze landed on us as we approached, but he
didn't bother to lose the joint that he held between
his fingers. Instead he took another drag and focused

his bloodshot eyes on me. I watched as they raked up my body while thick smoke spilled from his lips.

"What can I do for you, cutie?" he said to me as if Brant were nowhere in sight. *God, would I like to hit that.*

"*We're* here to ask you a few things." Brant said.

Craig took another drag of the joint and stared at Brant. "Well, what would that be then, looking to score a bit? What can I get you, a dime?" His eyes were back on me then, "An eighth?"

"That would be a big no." I said.

"Don't wanna get high, sweets?" *We could have a real fun time.*

"We were wondering what you were doing in the library last Thursday," Brant said, the tone of his voice dragging Craig's eyes to him.

"Last Thursday?" He took one last drag of the joint then tossed its remainder into the woods. "Who says I was in the library last Thursday?"

"I saw you there." I hadn't really, but it got his attention and he stood up and took a step toward me. His empty dark eyes with their red rims stared at me and refused to blink.

"That so, well then what is it *you* need to know? I'll let you have anything you want." He grabbed a piece of my hair and twisted it between his fingers. "What do you say, goldilocks, should you and I go for a walk?"

Before I could answer, Brant stepped in front of me and had his hand on Craig's chest. He pushed him back and I watched Craig stumbled for a step.

When he regained his balance, he stared Brant down with those lifeless dark eyes and I heard him think then that he wanted to fight him.

"Don't touch her," Brant said in a calm and cool voice. "Look, we think you're planning something, and we know all about it."

Craig looked startled. "Planning something? What are you talking about?"

"I'm talking about you wanting to kill things."

"Hey now, some stray cat..."

I felt my stomach twist.

"Not the cat."

"What?"

"I'm talking about students..."

Craig's face flared red with rage. "I'm not gonna shoot a person with my .22."

"What about a .22?" I piped in.

"That's how I killed that cat, got in my way when I was shooting cans in the backyard. It was an accident."

"I thought you skinned a cat?" Brant asked and Craig's eyes shot to him.

"What? Hell no, that's fucked up, man." Craig stepped up to Brant until he was a step away from him. Brant held his ground as Craig got in his face. "Look," he poked Brant in the chest with his pointer finger, "I don't know what you two are out here doing or what the hell you want from me, but whatever it is you're thinking, you're wrong." Craig's eyes were narrowed on Brant.

"Get out of my face," Brant replied, and that was

when I stepped up between them, throwing my hands up.

"Hey, stop now, Brant, let's go."

Brant wouldn't even look at me, and as I stood there I could hear both of them in my head. They were both waiting for the other to make a move, egging the other on in their thoughts. Then I put my hand on Brant's arm and he backed up a step with me.

Yeah that's right, back up, you chicken shit. Let your girl lead you away since you're not man enough to handle it yourself.

I cast Craig the dirtiest look I could muster and was glad that only I could hear his thoughts. Brant took another step back as I tried to pull him away from the impending fight. His frosty eyes remained pointed at Craig and his fist clenched at his side. I could feel his muscles twitch beneath my fingertips where I held his arm.

"Brant, please," I said and finally I felt his muscles give just a bit and he turned to walk away with me.

As we walked back towards school, we came up to a chain link fence. Brant kicked it. The fence shook and rattled, the metal links sounding like a dull chime. It seemed to have eased some of the tension that had been coiled up in his veins, but I could tell Brant was still angry.

Prick.

I stood a few feet from him, wanting to give him some space. "I really didn't like that guy."

"I still think it was him," he said and we continued walking back toward school.

"I don't know. He's a total creep, but he didn't have any idea what we were talking about, and he didn't sound right."

Brant sighed. "Damn, I really thought we'd figured it out."

"Yeah, me too."

He stopped walking and so did I. He turned to me, sighing again. His blue eyes were calm now and he opened his mouth to say something. I watched his lips slowly part. It was then that we both heard the loud screeching of Mrs. Farrow's whistle. I winced at the sound and turned to see her walking towards us. She was wearing a pink polo today, but she still looked rough and somewhat masculine.

God, I don't want to deal with this right now.

"What do the two of you think you're doing?" she asked as she approached us.

"We were just..." I began.

"Just nothing, you're supposed to be in class right now. Do either of you have a note or a pass?" Her eyes narrowed on Brant. *I know you don't*, she thought.

He rolled his eyes then looked down at her. Brant towered over Mrs. Farrow as she was a good six inches shorter than I was. Her size made her scowl and stiff posture far less intimidating.

"No," I sighed. There was nothing else I could say.

Brant didn't even bother to say anything. Mrs. Farrow had already pulled out her pink-slip notepad and was writing us up. She ripped the slip from the pad and shoved it toward us.

"The two of you can report directly to the principal's office."

Brant snatched the slip out of her hand crumpling it in his grip, and walked off. I followed.

We sat in the uncomfortable wooden chairs outside Principal Donohue's office. He currently was talking to another student, and so we were left to wait to hear our punishments. It was well into second hour now. Brant sat beside me, slouched in his chair with his head leaned back against the wall. He stared at the ceiling while I crossed and uncrossed my legs, unable to get comfortable. An air vent was directly above our heads and cold air poured down around us causing goose-bumps to form on my arms and legs.

I hate waiting, I heard Brant think, *always waiting, waiting now, was waiting yesterday, been waiting around for eight years*.

I turned to him then and the look he gave me was as if he just remembered that I could hear his thoughts.

Just stop thinking about it.

Mr. Donohue's office door opened. A girl with red hair and an excessive number of piercings stepped out. She ignored us as she left, swinging her black messenger bag across her shoulder. Across the room, the receptionist, a plump brunette woman with her hair pulled into a tight bun, nodded at Brant and I.

"You two can go in now," she said and we did.

We were both given in-school suspensions, and for the rest of the day were required to clean the desks in the detention hall. Mr. Donohue said if we were going to skip class that it was a fitting punishment to make us stay at school. He then added that if we were caught skipping again, it'd result in a Saturday morning detention. Brant didn't seem fazed by the threat, but the thought of spending even one Saturday at school was enough to make me never want to skip class again.

After getting to the detention hall, I realized that it wasn't such a bad punishment. Basically I traded a day of classes for cleaning. However, our punishment also came with a phone call home which I knew would be a lot worse. I tried not to think about the disappointment I'd later see on my mom's face. She'd start to worry if I was hanging out with the wrong crowd, might even think I'd started doing drugs. She always overreacted.

For a short while I focused on the task at hand. With a soapy rag in my grasp, I scrubbed at the profanities that had been scribbled on the desk before me in marker, pencil, and pen. Most of them would come up. Those that had been etched into the wood of the desk would not. I didn't realize that Brant had not chosen to do the same as me to keep himself occupied. It wasn't until I heard a soft chuckle tumble from his lips that I looked up and saw him sitting in the desk beside me. He wasn't cleaning it, wasn't doing anything, he was just watching me.

"Never had an in-school before, huh?" he asked.

"No, why?"

"You don't need to work so hard. They'll only check on us once an hour in between classes. So long as you're working then you're fine... the rest of the time though, you can just sit there."

"Oh," I set the rag down and dropped my hands to my sides. "Won't they notice the desks aren't clean?"

"The desks are never clean, you won't be able to get half that stuff up, and even if you do someone will just write on it again tomorrow."

"Right... so what do we do then?"

He lifted an eyebrow at me and I saw his lip curve up just ever so slightly. It was somewhat suggestive, but he wiped the look from his face almost as quickly as it had appeared. If he'd been thinking anything then, I hadn't been listening.

"Not sure, usually I'm in here with Skyler or Jason, or both of them and we find something stupid to talk about."

"So let's talk."

"'Bout what?"

I frowned, "I don't know, what's your favorite color?"

He raised his eyebrows. "My favorite color?"

"Alright, fine, that's kind of lame... you got anything better?"

He laughed then swiveled in his seat so that he was facing me. "How about... what kind of things do you like to do? And my favorite color is green."

I smiled. We talked for some time after that about your regular 'get to know you' kind of chit-chat. I told him that lately I'd been enjoying reading, particularly suspense novels, as well as watching chick-flick romances with my mom. He told me that he played guitar and enjoyed reading as well and was currently working his way through *Fear and Loathing in Las Vegas*. It was an easy conversation, the kind that flowed naturally; the kind where you didn't have to think of what to say next. I found myself really enjoying talking with him.

"So where did you go yesterday?" I asked watching as the light that he had in his eyes suddenly darkened.

His muscles tensed up and he looked away from me. Suddenly the silence of the room was deafening. I thought about listening in on his thoughts, but decided not to. This was something he needed to be able to tell me on his own. He deserved that privacy.

"You listening in?"

"No... but I was earlier when you were thinking that... that you were waiting yesterday, that you'd been waiting for eight years." He sighed. "I'm sorry, I know this is none of my business."

"You're right, it's not," he sighed again, "I was at the Westfield Shopping Square."

My brow wrinkled in confusion.

"When I was ten, I went there with my mom. She had errands to run, Dad was working, and being ten, they didn't trust me enough to leave me home alone and not have it burn down... so I got dragged along, and naturally I was bored out of my mind. We ran into Jason and his mom when we got there and so my mom and Mrs. Davis let us go off on our own."

"There was a skate park within walking distance, and I had my board in the car, so Jason and I went there. I was supposed to be back at the square by two. I'd promised her I'd be back on time." Brant's eyes looked glossy as he spoke, as if he were focusing on some imaginary point in the distance. "But we lost track of time, we were having too much fun. At about three, Mrs. Davis pulled up to the park and picked us up. She was a little mad that we'd been so absentminded, but I think she'd gotten caught up shopping as well so she didn't yell at us too bad.

"She drove me back to the Square and we all made our way to the fountain in the center where we were supposed to have met the hour earlier. My mom wasn't there. Jason's mom tried calling her on her cell. She didn't answer. We waited there another hour before Mrs. Davis just took me home. Mom never came home after that."

Brant looked at me with an expression I'd never seen him make. He looked soft, vulnerable. I stared at him, feeling a knot in my stomach twist, thinking about his pain and I noticed he had one freckle or maybe it was a birthmark just above his left eyebrow that was shaped like a tiny heart, but I only saw it for a second as he shook himself free of the memory and took a deep breath.

"Since then I've gone back there on the same day every year. It's stupid, I know. I don't actually expect to see her, but it... it makes me feel like I'm doing something." We were both silent for a while. "So yeah, that's where I was yesterday."

I couldn't offer him any real comfort, I knew that. "I'm sorry," I said even though I knew it didn't help. "I wish I knew what to say, but..."

"It's okay, I don't expect you to know what to say, I don't expect you to understand. Your parents are probably both still together and *living the American dream* or what have you."

I snorted, "Yeah right, they've got the *perfect* marriage," I looked away. "My dad's cheating on my mom. She doesn't know. No one knows... except me." I looked to him, realizing how personal of a thing I'd shared. I felt embarrassed, like I'd said too much and I wished that I could take it back. Quickly my eyes found the floor and I felt my cheeks growing red.

"I'm sorry," he said and we both nodded. "I didn't mean to assume..." He seemed flustered.

"I haven't told anyone that," I confessed. "I just...I heard him thinking about this other woman and it's like...like everything I thought about him is a lie. I don't know what to think about any of it, I don't know what to do."

He was nodding and had a faraway look in his eyes again. "I know what you mean. I wonder all the time where she is. Is she alive... is she dead, did someone take her, did she leave us? It's like I don't know who she is any more... I've never told anyone that either, I mean Jason and Skyler know that she... disappeared, but I don't really talk about it much anymore."

I wanted to ask more about his mom. I wanted to

know if they called the police. Did they file a missing person report? Did they ever find any clues to where she might have gone? I tried to think about what I would have done had it been my mom, tried to think of reasons that would have explained her disappearance. I couldn't. I didn't understand any of it. But despite my eagerness to know more, I could tell that this was a tough subject for him, so I kept my questions to myself.

I nodded. "Guess we both have our secrets."

14

Irresponsible

When I got home I found that it wasn't Mom I should
have been worried about. She was there with that
look of disappointment across her face. Her arms
were folded and her shoulders slumped as she sat at
the edge of the oversized brown loveseat, but Dad
was there as well. I walked into the living room and
found both sets of eyes on me. Dad was sitting on the
sofa. He had his hands folded in his lap and he and
Mom looked like they'd just been talking. He looked
at me. His gaze so strong that it pinned me in place
and then he stood up.

I hadn't expected to see him. He usually wasn't
home from work until dinner time or later, but then
again he usually wasn't really at work either. I
shifted my weight from one hip to the other, feeling
uncomfortable under his stare.

God, what is happening to my baby girl? I heard
Mom think.

"We need to talk," Dad said as I walked into the living room. He was still in his work clothes which made him look even more imposing and added to my anxiety.

I didn't sit down.

"We got a call from your principal today." He said.

"Yeah, I figured you would."

Mom was looking at me as if I'd just shaved my head and had been brought home by the cops. She looked like she was scared for me. "Honey, what is going on with you? You can talk to us."

"Mom, it's nothing, really."

"I don't call skipping school nothing." Dad said.

"Dad, really it's not how it sounds. I was on my way back into school..."

"I don't care what happened; you got an in-school suspension. That's not okay. You were being completely irresponsible."

"I'll catch up on everything I missed, it'll be fine."

"No, it's not fine. You were supposed to be somewhere and you weren't there."

"Were you doing drugs?" Mom interjected.

"What? No, Mom..."

"Ivy," Dad began again, "this is unacceptable behavior. From now on, you are not to go anywhere other than school for the rest of the week. After classes, I expect you to come straight home."

My skin burned hot and my cheeks flushed red with anger. "You wanna talk about not being somewhere you're supposed to be," my eyes burned holes into my father. Howard Randal Daniels returned the stare with equal intensity. "You're never here anymore. You're my father, you're supposed to be *here*... but you're always *working*, always away... we're your family, you're supposed to be responsible for us, so don't talk to me about responsibility... God, you're such a hypocrite, and you can't keep me here." I spun away from them and stormed toward the door.

"Ivy, don't you dare walk out that door," my dad yelled.

In the corner of my vision, I saw my mom stand up, one of the turquoise throw pillows falling to the floor. I walked out the door. Looking back, it was a fairly childish response, but it was all I could think to do. I had felt trapped, like a lion living like a housecat. Finding the person that was planning to blow up the school was higher on my priority list than going to class, but I couldn't tell them that. I couldn't explain what I had been doing or what I could do. They wouldn't understand. I also couldn't explain why I was so furious with my father, why I felt like he had no place telling me right from wrong. I couldn't confront my mother with that information. So I walked out the door slamming it behind me.

After that, I found myself driving more than a few miles over the speed limit. My fingers wrapped tightly around the steering wheel, the bones of my knuckles stretching the skin until it blanched white. I didn't know where I was going, I just needed to drive. I needed to get away. My mind raced as I drove on autopilot. I felt bad for running out of the house. I'd never done anything that disrespectful before, and yet I felt like my father didn't deserve my respect anymore. That was truly how I felt, but to think it sounded awful. He was still my dad, he still loved me and I still loved him even if I felt disappointed with him at the time. I just didn't know how to act around him anymore. My thoughts were conflicting and my head ached as I tried to sort them through. So distracted by the drama that was my life, I failed to notice where I'd driven to. It wasn't until after I'd passed the sign that read 'Laurel Hill Estates' that I realized where I was.

I was in Christy's subdivision, which was also Brant's subdivision, and I was nearing his house. For some reason my subconscious had directed me here. I tried not to let the Freudian psychology seep into my thoughts, trying to tell me that I secretly wanted to be here, but it got through anyway. It was then that I realized I was crying. Wet, hot tears rolled down my face, creating rivers through my makeup and smearing my mascara. They dripped from my chin and landed in my lap. His house came into view and I wiped my face with the back of my hand.

I was going to turn around. I didn't really want to see him. I certainly didn't want him to see me, not like I was. I was a mess. So I was just going to pull into his driveway and turn around, turn around and go straight home. I was going to apologize to my parents and forget about the fact that I had the lives of nearly a thousand students to save weighing on my shoulders, forget about the fact that I could read minds and knew that my father was having an affair.

I was going to shut myself off into a deep drowning pool of denial and go about my life like it had been before. Then he walked outside. My car was fully in the driveway. He had a full black garbage bag in his hand. For a moment we both froze. He stared at me and I stared back. Then, as quickly as I could, I put my car into reverse and started to back up. He dropped the bag and ran over to my car. I was halfway in the road when his hands came up to my window, palms flat against the glass. He called my name. I stopped, leaving my car half in the road. I rolled my window down and stared up at him and into his deep and concerned blue eyes.

"Ivy, what's going on?" *You look so upset.*

I tried to talk. My mouth opened but I was upset and my throat felt like it had swollen shut. The words refused to come out. I couldn't speak. So instead I sighed in frustration and shut my eyes, causing my tears to spill out onto my lashes and trickle down my face.

"Come on, get out of the car."

I did, and he got in. I stood to the side of the driveway with my arms crossed as if I were trying to hug myself while he pulled my car up to the garage. Then he made his way over to me.

"Hold on just a second, okay?"

His eyes were reassuring and I nodded. I focused on the chipping yellow nail polish on my toes which were peeking through my sandals and took a deep breath. Brant returned and put both his hands on my shoulders. The warmth from his hands on my arms was comforting.

"Come on, let's go inside, okay?"

I nodded. "Is your dad home?" I asked when we stepped into the kitchen.

He turned around to face me. "No, he's away on some conference for the rest of the week." He paused before leading the way down to his room. "Do you want anything, soda or something?"

"Um, Coke, if you have any." He walked over to the fridge and opened it up. I watched silently as he scanned the shelves.

Sprite, Mountain Dew, Pepsi.

"Pepsi's fine."

His head jerked to face me and he blinked, seemingly thrown off by the fact that I had just listened in on his thoughts. Then he grabbed a soda and popped the top for me.

"Sometimes I forget that you can do that. Here," he said handing me the Pepsi.

"Thanks."

He smiled and then turned to walk down the stairs. I took a sip of my soda and followed.

For a moment, as I stepped into the finished basement that was Brant's bedroom, I felt awkward. There were tingles of fear and uncertainty running through my veins as I thought about what would happen next. Here we were alone in his house, no parents, no friends, hanging out in his bedroom, and I was emotionally charged and feeling needy. In that moment, I actually understood the phrase 'butterflies in your stomach' as I felt like I had a swarm of them flying around in mine. Suddenly some-not all, but some-of my concerns with my parents and my abilities were forgotten as I became hyperaware of the fact that I was alone with a boy in his bedroom, a boy who, despite my previous dislike for him, I could not deny that I was attracted to, a boy who, despite his bad boy reputation, I found myself truly getting to know and liking for the person he really was.

"Ivy," he said, and I was shaken from my thoughts. He was standing before me. *I'm worried about you.* "What happened?"

"Sorry, I didn't mean to come here and..."

"Don't worry about it... just talk to me."

I sighed. "It's just stuff with my parents." I sniffled.

He brought his hand up to my face and wiped away a tear from my cheek with his thumb. His skin felt hot against mine. My eyes looked up at him wide and glossy with unshed tears.

God you're beautiful, I heard him think. Then he shook his head as if trying to keep me out, keep me from hearing his thoughts. His hand fell back down to his side and he turned to look back into the depths of his room.

"Let's sit down," he said when he turned back to me and I followed him over to the couch.

He cleared off the papers and notebooks that were scattered on the leather sofa and I sat down beside him. I took another sip of Pepsi then set the can down on the small end table beside me. Without the cold aluminum in my grip, my fingers felt restless.

My hands fell into my lap and I pulled at a hangnail on my thumb.

"It's my dad." I was still looking down, examining my fingernails as if they were the most fascinating thing in the world. "Mr. Donahue called home and..." I sighed. "They were both pissed. Mom was more worried than anything I guess, but Dad just wanted to punish me. He didn't even ask me what happened. He didn't even hear my side of the story, he just wanted to dish out my sentence so he could be done with it, no real parenting required." Even I could hear the resentment in my voice. "It was like he was mad that he had to leave work or his mistress or whatever to deal with his daughter.

"I feel like he was madder about that than anything I actually did. He told me I was being irresponsible," I laughed bitterly, "I was being irresponsible by trying to prevent someone from blowing up the school, right.... *Irresponsible...* And what makes it all worse is that I know he's cheating on my mom, but I can't call him out on that. I can't ground him or tell him that he's to come straight home after work instead of seeing that *whore*."

I bit my lip then. I was surprised by my own words. Finally my eyes flickered up to Brant and I saw him looking on at me intently. I felt the tears returning to my eyes and, as they welled up again, I ran my hands through my hair. That was when he moved to me and pulled me into a hug.

It's not fair, I heard him think and I began to sob uncontrollably.

With the anger released, all that I had left was pain.

He held me tight and shushed me while he stroked my hair. *I know how you feel.* He tried to calm me down. *I know what it feels like to feel alone, to feel like you have no one to lean on.* My tears began to ebb. His words of understanding were in my head and I felt his strong hands rubbing my back. He had me feeling like he was on my side, like I could lean on him.

I pulled away slowly, feeling the warmth drain from my body as the distance grew between us. His hands twisted away from my back and moved to my arms, rubbing them up and down. For a moment, as my face moved past his, my eyes fluttered down to his lips. I could feel his breath against my cheek, feel his comforting touch on my skin, and the butterflies returned to my stomach, swarming as if they were caught in a windstorm. I pulled back a little more, feeling the need to put more distance between his lips and mine. At that moment, I was far too focused on my own thoughts to even think about listening in on his.

"You okay?" he asked.

I nodded, "Yeah... yeah I'm fine." I took a deep breath. "I'm sorry, I didn't mean to come here and get all weepy on you."

He smiled. "Don't worry about it." He dropped his hands back to his sides.

I watched them fall, wishing they were still on my arms comforting me.

"I know how you feel. After... after my mom disappeared, Dad got real distant. I think he blamed me... sometimes I blamed myself. I'd think that if I had just stayed with her then I could have... stopped her, or protected her, or I don't know exactly but I would at least have known what happened to her.

"Maybe that's where you and I differ in all this. I feel alone because I need to know more, but you...you're alone because you know too much."

Our eyes met and we had a moment of understanding, a moment where just that look conveyed every emotion either of us needed to express-the sadness, the anger, and the regret of wishing we would have done something to change how things were, wishing that there was something we could have done.

He sighed. "You may think your dad is being out of line, that he doesn't have a right to tell you what to do with... with what he's doing, but he does care about you. Trust me, he took the time to come home and yell at you. If nothing else, that means he worries about you. My dad's never around anymore. When I get in trouble, I'm lucky if he even mentions it. He doesn't yell at me. Instead he just throws some money at the school and acts like that fixes it... Your dad still notices. That's something."

I offered him a wan smile. In that moment, I wondered if his bad boy reputation was a product of years of trying to get his father to notice him. I wondered if he picked up habits like drinking and smoking and skipping school in an attempt to get his father to yell at him, to get him to pay attention to him, to show him that he still cared. Brant's dad must have been a wreck after his wife disappeared, but he lost sight of the fact that his son was drowning. In that moment, I felt selfish for pouring my concerns onto him. My problems suddenly seemed much more manageable.

"Thank you," I said with true sincerity.

He nodded. "So what are you going to do now, with your dad?"

"I don't know. Go home and apologize I guess. Don't know if I'm quite ready for that yet though."

A large grin formed on his face and it made me smile. "Well then, looks like we've got some time to burn... how do you feel about Rummy?"

"You wanna play cards?"

"Yeah, why not? There's nothing on TV and it'll give you a reason not to go home just yet and will keep me from being home alone and bored out of my mind."

"Yeah sure," I said.

He got up and went to the dresser below the TV. In the first drawer he pulled out a deck of cards that were bound together by a thick rubber band. "You ever play before?"

"When I was younger with my Grandma I did."

"Well good, I don't have to go easy on you then."

We both smiled as he shuffled the cards.

An hour later, we were sitting on his bed. Each of us had cards in our hands. I was sitting cross-legged, focusing intently on what my next move would be.

Brant was lying on his side seeming confident that he
would win. After all, he had more points than I did,
but it was close. The game was coming to an end as
most of the cards were on the board, so to speak. I
laid down a four, five, and six of spades. I still had
one card left but no place to play it. Then it was
Brant's turn. He had two cards. My eyes went wide
as he laid down the three and the seven of spades,
successfully ridding himself of all his cards.

"Oh no," I squealed, "I was so close."

He laughed at me and then that mischievous
smirk I'd come to associate with him returned to his
face.

"It was a good game though."

"Yeah, so was the last one and I lost that one too."
He laughed again.

"It was fun though, got my mind off stuff."

"Well good, I thought so too. It was fun." His eyes
met mine.

His gaze had an intensity to it that made me feel
like I couldn't move. The air grew thick and for a
moment every breath I took felt like it was laced with
lead. In that moment, there were no thoughts, not in
my head or in his. All I could concentrate on was the
sudden pounding in my chest as if there were a
subwoofer there, pulsating to the rhythm of my heart
and making my whole body vibrate. Then he leaned
in toward me. It was a small movement and an
intuitive one, just a slow sway and slight tilting of his
head. It was then that my thoughts raced back to me.
I took a sharp intake of breath and snapped out of my

daze.

"Well I should, um... I should get going."

He blinked. "Right, yeah... yeah of course. I'll walk you out."

15

The Number Purple

Brant walked me to my car and we had an awkward moment just before I got in. Standing in his driveway, I felt like I didn't know what to do with any of my limbs. I crossed and uncrossed my arms, placed my weight on one leg then the other. Part of me wanted to hug him, thank him. Another part of me, and it was a small part that I refused to acknowledge at that point in time, wanted to kiss him. Instead I offered a nervous smile and drove home, all the while he watched me pull away.

My family was done eating dinner when I got home. Sadie was in the living room with Dad, watching TV. Dad refused to turn around. He refused to even look at me. I didn't listen to his thoughts. I didn't want to. So I waved to Sadie and walked into the kitchen. Mom was doing the dishes.

"Hey," I said.

She glanced back at me. Then she sighed and

continued scrubbing the casserole dish that was in her hand. "You missed dinner," she said without looking at me.

"I'm sorry."

She spun around, the casserole dish forgotten in the soapy water of the sink, and glared at me. "What's going on with you, Ivy? You're lying to me, skipping school...What happened?"

I sighed, "I'm sorry, Mom, I'm just... I'm going through something, I just... I can't explain. Just trust me, it isn't bad. I'm not doing anything that would make you disappointed in me, except skipping school, but I promise I won't do that again."

"Is it a boy?"

Brant's face flashed in my mind for a moment.

"Because if it is you can talk to me about it," she said.

"It's a lot of things, I think, but really I'm okay."

Mom walked over to me and pulled me into a tight hug. I welcomed her arms around me and hugged back. She kissed me on the forehead and looked down at me with enough worry in her eyes to circle the earth with.

Just, be careful.

The rest of the night Dad refused to speak to me. He and Mom seemed distant as well. They barely looked at one another when we were sitting in the living room watching a rerun of *Friends*. I decided not to listen in on any of their thoughts. It was easier not knowing things sometimes. Sadie came over to sit by me at one point and showed me the picture of our family she'd drawn for a class assignment. We all looked happy in her abstracted crayon representation. Later I wished Sadie goodnight as Mom took her off to bed and then decided to go up to my room myself. I said goodnight to my father. He didn't respond. I felt guilty that my disrespect to my parents had made him so angry with me that he didn't even want to acknowledge that I was there, but I also felt like he was being immature. I didn't know how to handle the way he was acting, so I just went to bed.

Mom peeked her head into my room shortly after I'd turned off my light. She told me she loved me and wished me goodnight. Before I fell asleep, I heard the murmured sound of voices coming from the living room. It sounded like my parents were fighting, but I couldn't make out what they were saying. I rolled over in bed and did my best to ignore it until I'd fallen asleep.

The next day at school, it felt like there was a buzz in the air, an energy floating about among all the students. I set foot on campus feeling good about myself for the first time in a long time. I felt like I was starting to get a handle on who I was. I walked onto the common smiling. It was then that I saw them across the way. Standing by the fountain that used to be my usual meeting spot with my friends I saw Christy. She was smiling as her hand was woven with Chase's. I watched as he leaned in and kissed her. I stopped smiling. My eyes were glued on them and I felt my heart drop into my stomach. It sat there like a rock in my belly, the weight of which made me feel nauseous.

I hope he's as into me as I think, I'm really starting to fall for this guy, Christy thought. Their kiss broke apart and she smiled up at him with a bright cheesy grin.

I felt heartbroken, and it was a strange feeling to wrap my head around. I had no reason to be upset that Christy and Chase were seeing one another. I had seen it coming and, furthermore, I hadn't ever had any kind of relationship with Chase. I wasn't even close with him. But I had built up this idea about him in my mind, built up an idea of who he was and that I had a chance to be with him. I had been perfectly fine living with the fantasy that something would come about between us so long as he was single. Now that I saw him there with Christy, my reality came collapsing down upon me.

What is she staring at?

My head spun around, my hair whipping in the air, and I saw Brant walk up behind me.

"Nothing," I said a bit too quickly and turned away from him.

He continued to look in toward where moments ago my eyes had been locked. I couldn't look back at them.

"You staring at Christy and Chase?"

I didn't answer.

"Hey, look at me, I can tell something's bugging you."

I turned around, but still I kept quiet.

"They're dating, you know." It was as if he said it to judge my reaction. "Heard about it from Skyler, guess Chase made some big show of asking her out at that pizzeria over on Fifth."

My lips thinned and my muscles tensed. I felt uncomfortable and Brant could tell.

"That is it, isn't it?"

"Brant, just leave it." I started to walk away, but he stayed right by my side.

"What've you got some crush on the football player?"

My eyes glared at him. They were angry and yet begging him to stop at the same time.

"That is it; you've got a thing for Chase Bryant."

"Brant, lay off."

He wouldn't. "I just... what do you see in him anyway?"

"Can we not?"

He looked at me, his stare harsh and serious. I could tell he knew I was upset, and the fact that he could see through me so easily only made me more upset.

"Sorry."

"It's fine... just forget it." The bell rang and I glanced over at the school as people started to shuffle off to class. "I can't miss any more classes or my parents are going to kill me so..."

"Right, yeah, I'll see you at lunch then, alright?"

"Yeah."

With that I left, throwing Brant one last glance over my shoulder. In the periphery of my vision, I saw Chase throw his arm around Christy and I winced. I rushed off to class, trying to ignore the irrational sense of heartbreak that had come over me.

Brant was by my side immediately after Bio. Like a magnet attracted to my polarity, he found me through the crowd within minutes after I stepped out of the Science lab. He said hey and I returned the greeting with a smile. Then we made our way out to the common. This was the first time we were ever together during lunch and actually going to lunch. It was strange. Not the being around him part, I was used to that. But he was usually helping me interrogate someone or annoying the hell out of me, or comforting me as I cried my eyes out. I shook the last thought away. What we hadn't really been yet was casual with one another. As I thought about that, I felt an awkward weight in the air between us as we stepped out onto the common.

Skyler and Jason waved to Brant from across the way. They motioned in a way to suggest that they wanted him to follow after them. Brant waved them off and they disappeared, walking toward the parking lot. Then he followed me to a table. We sat in the shade of a palm tree near the building and a good distance from my friends, a good distance from Christy and Chase who, at the moment, seemed to be tasting more of each other than their food.

I had made myself a lunch that day, feeling like I'd want more than a bagel to eat. Brant had nothing. He just sat down before me and folded his hands atop the table. I pulled the salami and cream cheese sandwich out of my brown paper lunch bag as well as an apple and a can of soda.

She's so much better than that meathead jock, Brant thought and I saw his eyes flicker over to Chase. *What does she see in him?*

If I didn't know better, I would have thought he was jealous. "So, what's our next move?" I asked and his face snapped to me.

Next move? He looked confused.

"With neither Eric nor Craig looking like our guy, we need a new suspect."

"Right, right... except..."

"Except you don't have anyone in mind?"

His lips thinned.

"Yep, and neither do I... so now what?"

He thought for a moment. "We need to go about this differently. Need to think out of the box."

I bit into my sandwich and looked at him expectantly. I had no ideas, nothing. I'd been kind of banking on him coming up with something.

"We've just got to narrow it down somehow."

"I was thinking that too... I just don't know how. That was when I talked to Charlie and..."

"Charlie?"

"Charlotte, the girl in the library... I just asked her if she remembered who had all been in the library that day, the only person that stuck out to her was Craig though. We could talk to her again maybe."

Brant's eyes lit up. "Actually yeah, we should, but I don't want to ask her about her memory."

My brow creased and I looked at him confused. "What are you thinking?"

"Like *you* have to ask."

"Actually yeah, I wasn't listening in."

He flashed me a cocky grin. "Guess it'll be a surprise then." He stood up. "Come on, let's go."

I took another big bite of my sandwich and grabbed my soda as I got up and followed after him. *So much for eating a decent meal*, I thought as we walked into the building.

The library was stuffy and as we entered I wished that I was still outside breathing in the fresh air. Charlotte, or Charlie as she had asked me to call her, was sitting behind the desk in the library eating what appeared to be a peanut butter and banana sandwich. I wondered if she ate in here during her shift every day, wondered if she always had lunch alone. It sounded lonely, but then again I'd been doing much the same lately.

Brant and I approached the desk. Her large brown eyes looked at us with a hint of embarrassment as she swallowed a bite of her sandwich and wiped the corner of her mouth with the sleeve of her red zip-up.

"Can I help you?" she asked.

Brant leaned against the counter, smiling down at her. He looked at her with a flirty gaze. I had to restrain myself from rolling my eyes.

"Just have a few questions... when I check out a book, that computer keeps a record of it yeah?"

"Yep." Charlie nodded.

Instantly I understood where Brant was going with this. It was so stupidly obvious. I was surprised neither of us had thought of it sooner.

"So if I wanted to, I could look back and see when I checked out a book, or maybe look and see who all checked out the same book as me. Maybe get a list of everyone who's checked out books on, say, bomb building?"

"Um… I can't give out other people's information."

"But you do have access to it yeah?"

"Sure, but… why are you asking me this?" *Bomb building, what is this about?*

"Look, Charlie, I know this all sounds weird but it's really important," I said, my eyes pleading with her.

"I don't know what you want me to say, giving out that kind of info is against the rules."

"Look," Brant started, "Charlotte, this is life or death here. Someone's going to try and blow up the school." He was being as serious as he could, but Charlie looked at him like he was about to tell her that she was on a hidden camera show.

Yeah right, "So why don't you talk to, I don't know, the principal or the police about it?"

"Well… we don't know who it is. That's why we need to look at your computer there, narrow things down."

"Right… and how do you know this?"

"I know this sounds crazy," I said then took a deep breath knowing that what I was about to say would have Charlie thinking I deserved to be in a mental institution, "but... I heard someone thinking about it... I can read minds."

Crazy? Try crazier than a June bug in May. Charlotte stared at me with a blank expression, and her eyes were screaming 'do I look stupid?'

"Crazier than a June bug in May," I repeated what I'd heard her think and watched as her eyes bugged out turning into deep wide pools of chocolate brown. Her brow creased and her jaw dropped open. She didn't believe me yet, but it was something.

"How..." it was at that moment that the bell rang and our conversation came to an abrupt end.

"Meet us after school," Brant said, "out the west door."

When I walked out the west door at the end of the day, Brant was already waiting for me. There was a cool breeze that drifted the smoky smell of barbecue past my nostrils and in the distance I could hear a dog barking and children playing. Brant threw the butt of the cigarette he'd been smoking at the ground and stubbed it out with the toe of his boot. In that moment I wished that I could be at some family picnic instead of searching for an unbalanced teen. Then Brant looked up at me. The bright afternoon sun shone on his face and lit up his features. Not for the first time, I felt myself being pulled deep into his eyes as the sun made them shimmer. Just then the nearby picnic and are wannabe bomber were both forgotten.

Ivy... His thoughts faded as if he were trying to

keep them from me. He seemed to be trying to keep them private a lot lately. I didn't think too much of it then. My mind wandered back to the situation at hand and I remembered that we were waiting to meet Charlie.

"Think I made a mistake telling another person about what I can do?" I asked.

He shrugged. "We need her help. If we could see who's been looking into the fabulous art of bomb building, that right there narrows down our search. She might even be able to look at the searches on the computers and see if any one username pops up with the most Google hits for the *Anarchist Cookbook*."

I nodded, and it was then that the door opened. Both Brant and I turned to see Charlie step outside. She eyed us warily, shifting the weight of her bag from one shoulder to the other.

"Okay, so you think you can read minds?" she asked. *Not that that's possible or anything.*

"It's freaky, I know, but we need your help," I said hoping that we could cut through her skepticism.

"So I'm just supposed to believe you and give out confidential information?"

"Oh come on now," Brant cut in. "These aren't medical records we're talking about, just a list of who checked out what book and when. 'Sides, why do you think we want them? What use would they be to us if we weren't telling the truth?"

She pondered his words, worrying a lip between her teeth. *I don't know what you'd really do with any of that information I guess. This can't be real though, can it? Could she really read minds?*

"Look, if you need some proof, I understand. I had to prove it to myself even. Just, um… think of a number, any number."

"And you're gonna guess it?"

"I'm going to tell you it, yeah."

Okay fine, guess this. Purple. I'm thinking of purple.

That time I couldn't help but roll my eyes. "Purple," I said.

Brant turned to look at me with a confused expression. "Purple isn't a number, Ivy."

I shrugged, "It's what she was thinking."

"Holy shit," Charlie said and we both turned back to face her. *There's no way she could have gotten that right. She can really read minds.* "This is really real."

I nodded, "Yup."

"Alright great, now that we're all on the same page, you can help us out yeah?"

Charlie seemed as though she hadn't even heard Brant speak. She was staring off into the distance and her mind was a jumbled mess of thoughts questioning everything she ever thought was impossible. I watched her twist a strand of hair around her fingers. Then I took a step toward her and placed my hands on her shoulders. Her distracted eyes focused on me.

"Look, I know this is really bizarre and you probably want some time to wrap your head around it, but we kind of need to know if you can help us."

Charlie nodded. "Yeah, well wait… you heard

someone say... or think that they want to blow the school up? Why?" *God, this is crazy.*

"I don't know why, all I know is that we have less than three weeks to figure out who wants us all dead and to stop them."

Brant let out a frustrated sigh. "Exactly, so can we go back inside and have you look up those book records up for us?"

Charlie frowned and twisted the hem of her sweater between her fingers. "Oh I can't right now. I will, but I have to do it on my shift. Mrs. Emmeric is working tonight and it's against the rules to do something like that."

"Okay, fine," I said. I wished that she could help us sooner, but I was glad that she was helping us at all. "So tomorrow?"

Charlie smiled. "Tomorrow, no problem, meet me in the library at lunch and I'll do whatever I can to help you find this guy... just don't tell anyone I'm doing this for you."

"Yeah, no problem. Oh and if you could not tell anyone about... well, me, you know."

"Oh, yeah no worries."

We parted ways after that and as I left the parking lot headed home I felt good. It felt good to be back on track, felt good to know what we were doing next. I started to think that we would actually be able to find this person that wanted us all dead and maybe even be able to stop him. But it also felt good to have another person know about my gift.

I hadn't realized how alone I'd been feeling until

that moment. I recognized then why I'd gone to Brant's house the night before when things with my parents started to weigh too heavily on my shoulders. He was all I had. I started to wonder if that was the only reason I'd subconsciously driven myself to his house. Memories of butterflies fluttering in my belly and the feel of his hot breath against my cheek rushed through my mind. I pushed those memories aside.

16

Down and Out

That night, I only saw my father for a few hours before I went up to bed. He still wasn't speaking to me, but I also still hadn't apologized. It was hard to do when I felt like he was being more immature about things than I was. For a short while, I started to wonder if maybe he was giving me the silent treatment because he felt guilty. Maybe the things I'd said to him had hurt. I was too afraid to listen in on his thoughts though, too afraid to hear that that wasn't the case.

Mom seemed to have softened up some. She was glad to see me when I got home and eager to hear about my day. She wanted to go shopping that weekend and was quite happy when I'd told her I was up for it. Spending more time with her, as it seemed, made her more eager to forgive me for skipping school.

The next morning, I slept through my alarm and

ended up getting to school just as the first hour bell rang. I looked around for Brant as I hustled into the building but I didn't see him. Knowing I had some catching up to do from my missed day of classes on Tuesday, I was wide eyed and ready to absorb everything my teachers had to say. I didn't regret skipping class, but I wasn't about to let it affect my grades either.

By lunch I felt like I had caught up on all my morning classes and that I could tackle my afternoon ones with ease. I was ready to get back to doing what I really cared about, and I felt like I could actually handle keeping up my grades along with searching for the bomber. For the first time, I felt like I had everything under control. At noon, I didn't even bother walking toward the common. I went straight to the library. On my way there, I met up with Brant in the hallway.

"Hey," he said and I grinned. "Where were you this morning? Playing hooky without me?"

"No, I just got here late... and I don't *play hooky*, I excuse myself from classes to attend to far more important things."

He laughed. "Keep telling yourself that."

His response made me smile. We walked into the library and saw Charlie's gaze fall on us, her eyebrows lifted in eagerness as she spotted us from behind the counter. She had a sympathetic smile on her face, and it was then that I noticed the other person behind the front desk. He was wearing a blue shirt and khakis and was doing something with her computer.

Sorry guys, I heard her think and wondered what had happened. We made our way over to her and I watched as she bit her lip as we got close. She seemed almost nervous.

"What's up?" I asked glancing at the older man in khakis who was currently running some kind of program on the computer screen.

"Not much," she said. *Can I talk to you like this?* She thought.

"Yeah."

Almost all our servers went down this morning. This guy's been here apparently fixing them, but I don't think he has any idea what he's doing.

"Can I still check out a book?" I asked but the tone of my voice alluded to the alternate meaning of my words. I wanted to know if she could still look up the book records on the computer.

"Yeah, you can check out a book no problem... I just have to do it manually." She held up a stamp. "Stamp the book, write it down." *I can't use the computer at all, can't search for books, look up records, nothing.*

"That sucks," my voice held an incalculable amount of disappointment.

"Yeah, you're telling me." *Working here is crazy boring without the internet.*

"How long will it be down for?" Brant asked.

"We should have 'er back up real soon, kids," the service man cut in, glancing back at us with a smile.

Not today, Charlie thought, *maybe not for a*

couple days. I'm just hoping that nothing crashed and that when they get it back up, the records are still there.

"Thanks anyway, Charlie." I offered her a wan smile. "Thanks for trying."

I'm really sorry. I'll try and look them up as soon as I can.

I nodded. "Well, I'll see you later then," I said.

"Bye Ivy... Brant." She waved and we turned and started to walk out.

Wait, she then thought and I stopped and glanced back at her over my shoulder. *Meet me after class, by the west entrance again. I've got an idea for something that might help.* I nodded then Brant and I left the library.

Outside our Psych room, Brant and I paused to talk in the hallway. He glanced around as if worried that someone were planning to listen in on our conversation then he turned his eyes back to me. I knew I had to fill him in on a few things. He hadn't heard what Charlie had been thinking. For an instant, his face was taut with frustration and possibly annoyance. I realized that standing there while Charlie talked to me through her thoughts, to him, must have felt like listening in on a conversation in another language.

"So, what's the rest of the story?" he asked.

"Computers are going to be down for a while."

Brant shook his head. "We're running low on time. Two weeks from Monday we need to have this all figured out or our graduating classes are going to get a lot smaller."

"Yeah, I know... Charlie thinks she has an idea though. We're supposed to meet her after class."

He nodded. "Well, let's hope it's a good one then."

17

How to Make a Bomb

After class, Brant and I walked out of the west entrance to find Charlotte waiting for us. Her fingers were picking at her nails, chipping away the cracked blue polish. She smiled at us as we walked out the door, her expression bright with nervous excitement. I watched as she shifted her weight from one hip to the other, turning out her blue Chuck Taylors so I could see the corners of a big star on the high-tops peeking out from beneath her jeans. Her enthusiasm was like the bubbles in a boiling pot of water, ready to spill over onto the stovetop at any moment.

"Hey guys."

"Hey... so, what's this idea you've got?"

Charlie seemed to suddenly flush with confidence. "Okay, so I was thinking... gasoline, bleach, gun powder... all common bomb building ingredients, right? None of them hard to get one's hands on... but if this guy wants to blow up the whole school, he's gonna need a lot of them."

"You wanna try and figure out if anyone's been buying bomb building ingredients in bulk?" Brant asked.

"That's a good idea," I said, "but where do we start? I mean no place is just going to give us their credit card receipts and say 'here you go'."

Charlie was smiling, a large self-assured grin stretched across her face. "Not unless you have access to them yourself."

Olsen Hardware was the only hardware store in town, and it just so happened that Charlotte Olsen's father owned it. It was possible that whoever was planning to blow up the school had gone to the *Wal-Mart* just outside of town, but Olsen's would have been the closest and most convenient place to get any bomb building ingredients. As we all drove there in my Scion, I hoped that this would give us the lead we so desperately needed. I hoped, whoever this person was, that he had already bought what he needed to build this bomb, and that he had done so at Olsen's.

Brant and I stood behind Charlie as she typed away on her father's computer. We were all huddled in his small windowless office at the back of the store. It was hot in the small space, and smelled like sawdust and fresh cut wood. I cast a nervous glance at the door. Its green paint was chipping and exposed the silvery metal underneath. I was worried that someone would walk in before we had the information we needed.

"So what if they paid in cash?" Brant asked.

"Then we're out of luck," Charlie responded. The tapping of her typing reverberated in the room, becoming an obnoxious and relentless sound. It made me nervous.

"Let's just hope they didn't do that... although there aren't too many kids at our school with credit cards."

"More than you'd think" Charlie said, "and it wouldn't have to be a credit card. Lots of kids have check cards or debit cards."

I nodded in agreement because I had a debit card. After that I just hoped that whoever this person was that they were stupid enough to leave a paper trail.

"Okay, found one."

"What is it?"

"Mrs. Pople apparently bought six large gas cans last week."

"There's a Nick Pople at our school, he's a senior." Brant said.

"Oh and Robert Maclin, Robb M, bought three containers of bleach less than a week ago. That's a lot of bleach for a high school kid."

"My mom's had the same container sitting under our kitchen sink for over a year," I said.

Charlie kept scrolling through the files on her dad's computer. Every time she found something that sounded suspicious, I wrote down the name. Anyone who either went to our school or was the parent of someone at our school that bought something like propane or fertilizer was written down, especially if they bought such items in large amounts. The only problem was that we had no idea what kind of bomb this person was planning to build, and we had no idea if the propane tanks that Mr. Davis bought were for his son's explosive endeavor or for a backyard barbeque this weekend. In the end, we had a list of about ten people that seemed most suspicious. Ten was an easier number than what we were dealing with before, but it still didn't seem small enough. Especially since it was possible that whoever was planning this wasn't even on our list.

"Sorry, guys," Charlie said as we exited the hardware store, "I thought that would be a little more telling."

"It was a good idea," I said, squinting into the afternoon sun. "And it does help. At least it gives us ten people that we should look at before anyone else."

"We need to get a look at those book rentals," Brant added.

Charlie dug her hands deep into the pockets of her zip up. "The school flags all Internet searches on stuff like bombs too, I can look at those. I just need the servers to come back up."

"Why don't they just block sites like that?" I asked.

"In case someone's doing a report or a speech on that stuff."

"That makes sense."

"So, what now?" Brant asked.

Charlie shrugged. "Food?"

There was a *Subway* on Fifth Street. As I drove us there, I gave my mom a quick call. I told her that I'd stayed after class to catch up on homework from skipping school and that I would be getting a quick bite to eat with friends before coming home. She was glad to have me check in, but seemed somewhat concerned when she asked if I was out with Christy and Tiana and I told her that I wasn't. I hadn't told her yet that I was no longer hanging out with them. I imagined her wondering if I'd fallen in with a new crowd, a bad crowd. And the truth was that maybe I was hanging out with a new crowd, but they weren't a bad one. I was starting to like Charlie, and Brant was good company. Maybe a bad influence in the way that he was part of the reason why I skipped school earlier in the week, but it was for a good reason. Also he stood up for me when Craig Fister started to get too pushy and creepy, and he was a good listener too, much better then Christy had ever been.

We sat down at a table near the window to eat our subs.

"So, what are we gonna do with this guy when we do find him?" Charlie asked.

"Try and reason with him," I said as I unwrapped my sandwich from its paper constraints, "tell one of the teachers about him, the police."

"Why don't we just do that now? I mean we could say that we know someone is planning something, like an anonymous tip or something. Or, since we know when this is going to happen, we could just call in a bomb threat on that day. They'd evacuate the school."

"Can't," Brant said, "it's too hard to do anything

anonymously anymore, they can track calls, look up phone numbers, and they'd probably think we were involved just for suggesting it. Same with calling in a bomb threat, that's the best way to be suspect number one. It'd be different if we had a way to explain how we know what we know, but we can't... Once we know who it is then at least we can lie, say we overheard him talking about something, though that's not the best excuse."

"People probably say they'd like to blow up the school just about every day," I said, "doesn't mean they actually plan to."

"Right, so we need some proof, and good reasons to explain why we're not involved. I'm just hoping that's easier to figure out than who this guy is."

Our conversation quieted down for a short while as we ate. Homicidal teens were no match for hungry bellies. When you're seventeen, food wins out over serious conversation every day. After a short while though, Charlie's questioning picked up again.

"Who do you think it is?" Charlie asked.

"Hopefully someone on our list," Brant responded as he took a bite of his sandwich.

"I don't know," I said. "It could be anyone. Could be someone we see every day. Someone who's gone to school with us for years that we just never noticed, never paid any attention to... or maybe we did notice them, maybe it's someone I've picked on, or you." I looked at both Charlie and Brant, "Or someone who's been picked on and we just stood by and watched... Whoever they are, they feel this way because of us, because of people at our school. It makes me feel kind of sorry for them."

Charlie nodded in agreement.

"Not me," Brant said, "I don't feel sorry for anyone who's trying to kill me. Everyone gets picked on, we all feel alone sometimes. I don't care if you're Eric Thompson or Christy Noonan, we all feel alone, feel left out, looked down on. Everyone gets talked about behind their back, but we don't all go out on killing sprees. Whoever this guy is, whatever he's been through, that doesn't make what he's doing right."

He took another bite of his sub and I let his words soak in. I thought about what it would take to drive me to kill someone, thought about what someone would have to say to me or do to me to push me to the point where I wanted them dead. I couldn't come up with anything. I understood what Brant was saying. Being picked on didn't excuse whoever this was, he was still responsible for what he was doing.

My mind mulled over Brant's words, but then the sight of something across the street jostled me free of them. My eyes became cemented to the window; my sub sandwich was momentarily forgotten. Across the street was Oregano's Pizzeria, and standing outside its doors were Christy and Chase. He was twisting a piece of her blonde hair in his fingers and she was looking at him with the brightest grin.

"Ivy, you alright?" Brant asked me and my eyes snapped back to him.

I watched as he looked out the window to see

Christy and Chase.

Charlie was looking that way as well "You're friends with her, yeah?" Charlie asked me.

"Not anymore… least I don't think so."

I wonder why, she thought but she didn't voice the question aloud. For that, I was grateful.

She's still caught up on that tool, Brant thought. His eyes were glaring out the window. *I just don't get it.*

"So, what are you guys doing this weekend?" Charlie asked and I was glad for the change in subject. I didn't like the fact that it bothered me that Christy and Chase were seeing one another, but I couldn't help the fact that it still stung.

"I'm going shopping with my mom tomorrow after school," I said. "You wanna come with us?"

"No, thanks, but I've got a thing… I teach guitar lessons to a few kids in the grade school Friday afternoons. Maybe another day this weekend?"

"Yeah, that'd be fun. I don't have any plans for Saturday, what about you Brant?"

"I'd be up for something."

"Here, lemme get your number," Charlie said pulling her phone from her pocket. I did the same. As I told her my number, Brant grabbed my phone and began to type his number into it. I didn't mind. As he did, though, I listened in on his thoughts and they weren't about me.

Guitar lessons, hmm. I'll have to see if the girl can really play.

I felt a sinking sensation in my belly. It wasn't

that I liked him; I shouldn't have been bothered if he
was expressing interest in someone else. And it
wasn't that he was even doing that. He played guitar,
it was only natural that he'd be interested in the fact
that Charlie played too. For a second then, I thought
about asking Charlie to teach me how to play
something.

"Alright, I'll text you," Charlie said and went
about typing in her phone. While she did, Brant slid
my phone back to me. A moment later, my phone lit
up with her text message and I saved her number.

"Well, we should probably get going," Brant said.

We were all finished eating and left shortly after
that. I dropped the both of them back off at school
and went home for a quiet night to myself.

18

You Learn a lot from Listening

That night, as I was lying in bed, I found it hard to fall asleep. I twisted and turned, flipping from one side of the bed to the other. My sheets got caught around my ankles, winding into knots. I tried sleeping on my back, then my side. Nothing felt comfortable. My queen-sized bed suddenly felt too big for me. It was like I was swimming in a sea of blankets. I had always liked to spread out as I slept and usually took up all available mattress real estate, but that night I felt like no matter how I laid nothing felt right. It felt cold and empty as if I was lying on the immense, bare surface of the moon.

Turning on to my side again, I spied my phone sitting on my side table. It was plugged into the charger and blinked a tiny green light at me. I stared at it for a moment then shut my eyes, but I could still feel the illumination of its green light against my eyelids. My eyes snapped open and I rolled onto my back, then with a sigh I grabbed my phone off the nightstand.

I began scrolling through my contacts, and stopped when I came to 'Brant Everett'. I paused for a moment, looking down at my screen which had his name lit up. I realized then that I had his number, but he didn't have mine. I almost set my phone back on the nightstand and tried to force myself to sleep again, but I didn't. I clicked his name and typed a text message.

'Hey, this is Ivy,' I typed. My finger hovered over the send button for what seemed like an hour. Finally, I hit send. I set my phone back on my nightstand and turned onto my side and tried to sleep. Just because I messaged him didn't mean he'd respond. After a few minutes, though, I heard the low buzzing that was my phone on vibrate. I turned over and grabbed it. Lying on my side, I looked at the message.

'Hey, what r u up 2?' his message read.

'Nothing, can't sleep, you?' I responded then left my phone beside me in bed.

After a few moments, it lit up again.

'Nm, was playing guitar.'

'What can you play?'

'Lots, I'll play u something sometime, u play anything?'

I thought for a moment. Mom tried to get me into piano lessons when I was younger but it hadn't stuck. 'No,' I said.

'Maybe I'll teach u something.'

When I got that text, I felt the iconic butterflies return to my stomach. It was that feeling of being so excited that you were short of breath, a giddy tingling feeling deep down in the pit of my belly. The butterflies fluttered about, and finally I realized that I kind of liked Brant Everett. I liked him in a way I never thought I would. We texted back and forth for some time after that. I told him about how my dad still wasn't talking to me, and he told me that his dad's business trip was getting extended. As we texted, I finally felt my body relax. Sleep finally sounded like a place I could reach, but as we talked, the last thing I wanted to do was to end our conversation. As it got later, however, I found my eyelids growing heavy and the need to sleep starting to overcome my want to text.

We finished talking about what music was currently in our iPod playlists, his being a mix of alternative rock including bands like *The Calling* and *The Black Keys*. Mine was a mix of classic rock including *The Outfield* and *Bryan Adams*. Then we said goodnight and I floated off to sleep with ease.

The next morning at school, I ran into Charlie as I walked onto the common. She and I talked until the bell rang. Mostly our discussion consisted of idle chitchat about what classes we were taking and what we thought of our teachers. I looked around for Brant at one point and saw him standing against the side of the building with Skyler and Jason. Our eyes met for a brief second and he gave me a short wave. I felt the sinking sensation return to my belly that had been there when I heard him thinking about Charlie the other day. It bothered me that he didn't come over to say hi. I had gotten used to talking with him in the mornings. I suppose I forgot that he had other friends.

Classes went by fast that day and lunch, for once, was just lunch. Brant and I had looked over the list we'd made when we met up halfway through the day, but there weren't any names that stood out to us. It was hard to know what to do next, who to talk to. We didn't know where anyone on our list would be during the lunch hour. And, it seemed, no matter how many times my eyes scanned the crowd on the common, I never saw any of the people we were looking for. Those ten people could have been hiding just beyond my sight, or they could have gone out to lunch as a number of them were seniors. Possibly a few of them were in the gym playing basketball. I was pretty sure that at least one of them was on the basketball team, another was a football player. Maybe some of them were in the library, or skipping school. Wherever the ten people on our list were, we didn't see them, but in truth we didn't look for any of them very hard.

Brant and I sat down. He'd gotten a small personal pan pepperoni pizza from the lunchroom and a Mountain Dew. I hadn't made myself a lunch that day so I bought a chicken Caesar wrap and grabbed a bottle of lemonade. We didn't talk about our texting from the night before, nor did we discuss in any detail the doom that awaited our school in a little over two weeks. Instead we talked about our

favorite movies and discovered we both had a love for
comedy zombie flicks such as *Shaun of the Dead* and
Zombieland. Then we talked for another twenty
minutes, discussing if either one of us would survive
a zombie apocalypse. I had insisted that I would live
longer than Brant since I could use my gift to hear
the zombies coming before they got to me. He,
however, shot down that idea, arguing that zombies
didn't have thoughts.

It was refreshing to have a silly, lighthearted
conversation with him. It almost made me forget that
I was the only thing that stood between the school
and its total destruction. Just before we parted to go
our separate ways for the rest of the day, he smiled
at me and it made me feel warm. It was one of those
rare moments of true comfortable silence

After class, I was walking to my car when I heard
something that made me stop. Ahead of me, Christy's
hair flapped in the wind. She held her cell phone to
her ear by wedging it between her face and shoulder
and dug through her Coach backpack. She'd stopped
walking in the middle of the parking lot. I thought
about walking past her and just going home, but for
some reason I stood there and listened in.

"Why can't I just bring him to dinner tonight?"
Christy said into the receiver.

I wanted to know who she was talking about so I
listened in on her thoughts. I wasn't sure if I'd be
able to hear whoever was on the other line speak, but
I tried anyway.

Because tonight we have to go shopping to get you

something to wear to the Play in the Park.

Organizing this event is really important, Christy. It was Christy's mother's voice that I heard. As Christy listened to her mother's words, I was able to hear them in her head.

"I thought we were shopping next weekend?" Christy said pulling her datebook from her backpack.

We had to move the event up so there's not going to be time next weekend. I'm sorry, Christy. I'm glad you have this boy you want me to meet, but you need to remember you have to keep...

"College in mind and make sure I get the grades and have extracurricular activities like community events and clubs on my application, and yeah, I get it Mom, I just..."

Just nothing, school and The Play in the Park *first, we'll talk boys later.*

The Play in the Park was an event we had every year. Students in the Drama department at the local community college would put on a performance with the kids in the community in mind. Last year, they did *Peter Pan.* This year I heard they were doing *Alice in Wonderland.* Mom and Dad would take Sadie and me to see it every year. We'd go early to get a good spot and lay out a blanket in the grass then fill up on carnival food like corn dogs and cotton candy. They always hired kids from the high school to work the booths, selling tickets and food. Christy's parents organized it. Her dad was a board member on the Community Council, so I always had Christy to hang out with when we went.

*Now there's going to be an assembly at your
school on Friday the fifteenth and I want you to help
your father talk to the kids at your school about
working in the booths and getting their families to
come. I want to have a better turn out than last year.*
Christy's mom continued on the other line, but soon I
heard Christy's own thoughts louder than the echo of
her mother's in her mind.

*God, sometimes I swear you ask me to meet these
absurd expectations to keep me from having a
boyfriend,* Christy thought. *All my friends are on the
honor roll, we all play varsity sports... well except Ivy
but who knows where she's been lately. Now I finally
find a guy that I like that meets all your
requirements... I mean how many guys on the
football team get a 3.8 GPA and go to our church?*

Christy, are you listening to me?

"Yeah, I'm here, sorry."

Her mother sighed. *Alright, well I'll see you when
you get home. Love you, sweetie.*

"Love you too, Mom, see you soon. Bye."

I watched as Christy hung up her phone and put
her datebook back into her bag. She closed her eyes
for a moment, taking a deep breath then walked to
her car. I stood there watching her as she drove
away. I always knew that Christy's parents pushed
her to succeed, but I never before realized how they
expected excellence from her in every part of her life,
including the friends she chose, the boys she dated,
the way she managed her time. For the first time, I
realized why Christy judged everyone around her the

way she did. She had to surround herself by people who met her mother's standards or she herself wouldn't meet them.

I went home after that to meet my mom for our shopping date. She was already waiting for me when I walked in the front door. Immediately, I raced up the stairs to leave my school bag in my room and grab a light jacket. We left shortly after that. As we drove to the mall, I was glad to have a day with her. It would be just the two of us as Sadie was being babysat by the neighbor, and Dad, as usual, had yet to come home.

At the mall, we bounced from one store to another, commenting on what we thought was cute and what we considered total insanity in the world of fashion. We talked about which decade fashion would be replicating next, would we see more neon and black in an 80's resurgence or were leather and metal studs making a comeback. Mom insisted that a good leather jacket never went out of style. I agreed and that was when she turned the conversation to what she really wanted to talk about-me.

"So how have Christy and Eliza and Tiana been? I'm surprised you didn't invite them shopping with us."

The shopping bag in my hand suddenly felt as if it had been filled with cement. I took a deep breath and thought about how to answer her question. It was hard to talk about some of the things that were going on in my life, being able to hear voices the hardest of them, but I felt like I'd been lying to my mom a lot lately and the urge to tell her the truth about some of those things was overwhelming.

"I'm kind of not really friends with any of them anymore."

Mom almost stopped walking in surprise but managed to keep her cool. She had a way of carrying on a conversation in a normal carefree kind of way, even when someone had said something that should be cause for alarm.

"What happened?" she asked calmly.

"We just… I don't know, I guess I just realized that they weren't the best friends. I started hanging out with a new friend, this guy, Brant… and they didn't approve."

A boy, well that makes sense, "I see. Honey, I know you probably think this guy means a lot to you, but you shouldn't ignore your friends because of him."

I laughed a short laugh.

"It's not like that at all, Mom. They stopped being friends with me because I was hanging out with him."

Mom sighed. *Girls can be so cruel. God, if I could see those girls now…*

'It's okay though," I said. "I've met some new people."

"I'm really sorry." She paused for a moment.

The sugary, sweet smell of cinnamon rolls drifted through the air as we rounded the corner to walk past the *Cinnibon*. I stared at the pastries through the window in the shop as we walked by.

"So who are these new people you've been hanging out with?" *I really hope they're not the reason why she was skipping school.*

"Well there's this girl Charlotte I met in the library. Mostly I've just been hanging with her and Brant."

"Brant? Is he your boyfriend?" She was trying to keep the conversation casual, but worry was slipping into the tone of her voice.

"No, Mom, we're not seeing each other. Just friends."

She sighed, possibly in relief. I, however, was running over my own words in my head. It was the first time I'd actually called Brant a friend aloud and the word felt right. We were friends. What was bothering me was that I was starting to wonder if we were something more.

"And, don't worry," I continued, shaking the thoughts of Brant from my mind, "neither one of them are the reason why I skipped school on Tuesday. Actually Brant was walking me back to school when I got caught."

"I really wish you'd tell me why you skipped class."

I looked at her, painfully aware that she was more concerned for me than she'd ever been in my entire life. I wanted in that moment to tell her everything, tell her about my ability, about someone wanting to blow up the school, about Dad's affair, but I couldn't. That was still something I didn't know how to say.

"I was just going through something, I needed some time to figure some stuff out, that's all. I promise you that you don't have to worry about me."

She reached over to me and pulled me against her as we walked. She gave me a tight squeeze then let me go.

"I love you, honey, and I'm glad you told me about all this."

"I'm glad too, Mom," I said, and I really was.

19

Everyone has Something

Saturday morning, Mom made waffles. Sadie and I sat at the breakfast counter to eat and Mom turned cartoons on the small TV in the kitchen. I smiled, watching as my little sister completely missed her mouth with a forkful of syrupy waffle because her eyes were glued to the screen. Dad came down the stairs. He was in his workout clothes and had a duffel bag slung over his shoulder and tennis shoes in his hand. Sadie jumped in her seat as he entered the room.

"Dad!" she shouted, her breakfast forgotten.

"Hey, kiddo."

"Can we go to the park today, please?" She dragged out the 'e' in her 'please,' begging with the best of her ability.

Dad smiled at her and ran his hand through her hair, ruffling it on her head. "Maybe later, ask me when I get back from the gym."

"Okay, I will."

Dad smiled again then grabbed a water bottle out of the fridge. He glanced at me.

"I love you girls, both of you," he said then started to walk out of the kitchen.

I thought about the awkwardness that had been between us lately and, just before he was out of the kitchen, I swung around on my stool to face him.

"Dad," I said and he stopped and turned around. "I'm sorry."

He nodded and offered me a soft smile. He looked happy to hear my apology, then I could see something resembling pain or regret enter his features, his eyes squinted and his jaw flexed. It was just a moment, a flash, like when you catch the cue mark in the upper corner of a film at the movie theater. That tiny black dot that's there one minute then gone the next. I wasn't listening to his thoughts, but I knew him well enough to read the emotions on his face, he felt guilty.

"I'm sorry too, kid," he said. Then he turned and left.

The rest of my morning and most of my afternoon was fairly uneventful. I watched cartoons with Sadie, helped Mom fold laundry, finished all my homework. A little after two, Charlie called me to see what I was up to. As it turned out, we were both rather bored and so we decided to see a movie. She met me at my house around four, and pulled up in a baby blue Chevy Lumina that was at least ten years old but appeared to be running well. Charlie made her way up the steps and Mom took a break from washing the dishes to come to the front door when she knocked.

I opened the door to greet Charlie. With Mom hovering behind me, I knew she wanted to be introduced so I invited her in.

"Come on in," I said. "This is my mom."

Mom stepped forward and said hi. Charlie grinned politely.

"I'll be just a minute," I said. "I'm just gonna grab my purse."

I was quick running to my room and grabbing my bag. When I came back down the stairs, Mom was in full parent mode as she asked Charlie about where she was planning to go to college. I heard Charlie tell her that she was planning to apply to UCLA but that her dad wanted her to go to Berkeley. Mom seemed pleased with her answers.

Seems like a nice girl, though she really should dye her hair all one color, Mom thought.

"Well we're gonna book," I said and then Charlie and I were out the door.

"Have a good time girls," Mom yelled as we walked to my car, and I waved back at her.

We picked a suspense thriller entitled *Crash*, and after it ended, we discussed the overdone CGI as we walked back to my car. The sun was beginning to set and the horizon was growing dark as the sky was cast in shades of red and purple. The shadows were reclaiming the sky, and slowly the last shimmering rays of gold melted into the abyss like a man's dying breath dissipating into the air. It was then that I felt the vibration of my phone ringing. I pulled it from my pocket and noticed that I had a text message. It was from Brant. I clicked it.

'If ur not doing anything u should come over, bring Charlie if u want.'

"Who's that?" Charlie asked.

"Brant, he wants to know if we want to go over to his place and hang out." I was suddenly nervous that Charlie wouldn't want to go.

Charlie thought it over for a moment. "Sure, if you want to."

"Yeah, why not?" I said casually, but inside I was tingling with excitement.

After that, I called my mom while we made our way over to Brant's house. She must have been impressed with Charlie since she barely even asked what we were up to when I said I'd be out later. She tended to be a lot less concerned about what I was doing when she liked the people I was hanging out with. She just said that she expected me home before midnight and to have a good time. We got to Brant's not fifteen minutes later.

I checked my hair in the rearview mirror before getting out of the car, frantically trying to flatten all the frizz. After parking in Brant's driveway, I felt unexpectedly nervous, as if maybe I'd swallowed some uncooked cornels of popcorn at the movie theater and they were now popping in my stomach. There was another car in front of mine that I didn't recognize and I wondered who all was here. Was Brant planning to have a party? I wasn't sure what to expect, but I was excited to see him nonetheless. Charlie followed me around the house and we let ourselves in through the sliding glass door.

"Brant?" I called out as I started to walk down the stairs to the basement.

He didn't answer but I could hear voices. I rounded the corner coming out of the stairwell. The room was void of smoke, but the smell still lingered like it was made up of burrs. The hooks of the smoke seeds clinging to the fabric and walls and getting stuck in your hair like little balls of Velcro. I saw him then, sitting on the black leather couch. Skyler was at the other end of it and Jason was sitting on the floor. A bottle of Jack Daniels sat on the coffee table. It was open but little had been drunk from it thus far. Brant's eyes locked onto me the second I came into view. He smiled and then he stood up.

"Ladies, come on in," he said.

I glanced back at Charlie and she and I walked into the room. Brant gave us his spot on the couch and leaned up against the wall as we sat down.

"Hey, I'm Skyler," Brant's friend said, giving Charlie a wave.

"I'm Jason."

"Charlie."

"And we all know you, Ivy," Jason said. *Brant's been spending a lot of time with you lately.*

"Hi, guys," I said, feeling my cheeks blush slightly.

"We, uh, we were thinking about playing cards or something," Brant said. *I'm glad you came.*

I smiled. "I'd be up for some cards."

"Great."

"I vote for a drinking game," Jason said as he grabbed the bottle of Jack off the coffee table.

Charlie cast me a nervous glance. "I-I don't know..."

"Oh, no worries," Jason continued, "there's no pressure, I'm fine drinking by myself if you're not feeling like it." He took a swig from the bottle and smiled at us. *Let's just have some fun.*

Charlie shrugged, seeming a little more at ease.

"I say either Kings Cup or Circle of Death," Skyler said.

Jason rolled his eyes. "They're the same thing, numbskull."

Brant was laughing as he grabbed the deck of cards. It was the same one that he and I had played Rummy with nights ago. He shuffled them in his hands and I watched as his fingers moved with precision as they bent the cards into an arch then let them fall back down in a crisscrossing pattern.

"How about poker?" Brant asked.

Skyler's eyes brightened. "Strip poker?" he asked.

"No, come on, Skyler, don't be a dick," Brant said then glanced at Charlie and me.

"Kidding, I was kidding." *Jeez, lighten up.*

"I don't know how to play poker," Charlie said.

"How about Crazy Eights then?"

She smiled and Brant shuffled the cards one last time.

"Crazy Eights it is." He dealt out the cards and

took a seat on the floor across from me.

The game was started in relative silence. We focused on the cards in front of us, planned our strategies. I laughed as Jason decided that every card he had to pick up constituted him needing to take a drink. After he had to pick up five cards in one turn, which translated into five swigs of whiskey, I heard Brant think that he was an alcoholic. The thought was joking but it also seemed to have some truth behind it. He set the bottle down after that and didn't pick it up again for some time regardless of if he had to pick a card or not.

Jason looked a little sick. *Ugh, that stuff burns. I really should mix it with Pepsi next time.*

Skyler shook his head at him. "That's what you get for drinking too fast." He grabbed the bottle and took a sip himself but set it right back down. *I wonder if I should offer them any.* He glanced over at us.

I softly shook my head 'no' and he didn't say a word.

I don't know if I knew exactly why I wasn't drinking. Maybe it was because I knew Charlie was uncomfortable with it and I didn't want her to feel singled out or alone. Then again, Brant didn't seem to be drinking either. Maybe it was because I was driving home, even though that hadn't stopped me in the past. I'd driven home after drinking at Nicolette's party only about a month ago.

I'd like to think my choice that night was based at least partly on the guys around me and how they

made it easy to say no. They didn't make me feel
pressured to conform or like I wouldn't have fun if I
didn't drink. In that moment, I thought about how
insanely stupid I'd been to drive home from
Nicolette's. I hadn't planned to drink that night, but
Christy had handed me a beer as she dragged me
down to the beach with the guys and made me feel
like I couldn't refuse. It was odd how sitting here
with Brant, Charlie, Skyler and Jason, I felt more
comfortable to be me then I ever did with Christy,
Eliza and Ti. What it came down to was that I simply
didn't want to drink, I was having fun just playing
cards, and that was fine with them.

"Hearts," Brant called as he laid down an eight.

I cringed. I only had one heart, a two. I set it
down and hoped that someone would change the suit
again before it got to be my turn. When I looked to
him, I saw he had that smug smirk plastered on his
face.

Out of hearts.

My eyes went wide. He laughed.

*I don't need to read minds to know what you're
thinking, Ivy. You'd make a terrible poker player.*

I laughed. He was probably right.

To my left, Charlie was giggling and holding her
cards to her chest as Skyler tried to peek at them.
The bottle of Jack that sat on the table appeared to
have been completely forgotten by this time.

Charlie won that game, but Brant placed a close
second. I watched Charlie smile as I offered to help
clean up, then as I reached for the cards that were

laid out on the coffee table, my hand brushed against Brant's as he did the same. We both jerked back from one another and our eyes met. He'd touched me before, grabbed my arm to stop me from walking away, hugged me, wiped a tear from my eye. But something was different now. That small contact between his skin and mine had my heart sounding like the metrical tapping of a dozen marbles that had their jar overturned at the top of the stairs to bounce over every step in an erratic rapping beat.

Sorry, he thought, but shook his head as if realizing that he had nothing to apologize for.

Brant smiled at me and went back to grabbing the cards off the table. I just watched. I overheard Charlie talking with Jason. They were arguing over something frivolous, and as they talked I found I was still watching Brant clean up.

"I'll prove it," Jason said, "Brant, mind if we use your kitchen? You've got bananas, yeah? I know there's pickles up there."

"Not positive about the bananas, but yeah go ahead."

Jason stood up then and started to walk out of the room. He nodded at Charlie to follow him and she did after casting me one last glance as if to double check that I'd be alright without her. Once they made it to the stairs, Skyler stood as well.

"Oh, I'm coming," Skyler said. "Maybe I can score a free sandwich out of this." He vanished up the stairs and then Brant turned to face me.

"You two having fun?" he asked as he put the

cards away in the top drawer of his dresser.

I nodded. "Yeah, yeah it's been fun... your friends seem nice, they're funny."

"Jason's just drunk, he's far less entertaining when he's sober," Brant joked sitting down on the couch beside me.

I laughed. "Does he always drink so much?"

Brant glanced at the stairwell for a moment as if to assure himself that we were alone in the basement. "Not usually," he said, "but he found out his little brother has cancer. Lymphoma... it's not as bad as it sounds, they found it early. He's got a really good chance, but Jason's been having a hard time with it."

All I could do was nod. I thought about what I would do if anything happened to Sadie, what I would do if she was sick. My little sister could be a real annoying brat at times, but I still loved her. If there was even the possibility of anything happening to her, I'd be devastated. I could understand Jason's need to wash away those feelings with the fiery liquid he'd been drinking that night. I knew what it was like to want to forget that something had happened to you.

"I guess everyone has something," I said and Brant smiled at me.

"I think people like to think that when something bad happens to them that they're special or something, as if no one else has issues in their life."

I nodded. I'd done the same thing when I found myself being able to hear people's thoughts. I wondered *why me*, but it wasn't just me. Everyone has something.

"So what's Skyler's story?"

Brant laughed. "Actually, not much. Nothing as obvious as a family member with cancer at least. He just likes to smoke. Smart guy though, could be the next President if he wanted, and as President his first official ruling would be to make marijuana one hundred percent legal, *no more of this medical excuse crap*, as he'd say." Brant laughed.

"Do you smoke?" I inquired and his eyes snapped to mine, wide and nervous.

"No... I mean yes, I mean, I have, but I don't." *God, you're a fumbling idiot, just talk to the girl.* "I've tried it, but it's not my thing."

I nodded. "I noticed you weren't drinking tonight either, so... what *is* your thing?"

I suddenly realized that we were sitting with little distance between us. His arm was casually resting atop the back of the couch, and he was turned to face me. Our knees were touching and the small amount of my skin that brushed against his jeans was tingling. I saw his sight waver from my eyes down to my lips, his long lashes fluttering at me. His lips were parted and I realized that mine were as well. I felt like I could feel every inch of my body. I was hyperaware of the slow shallow breath that passed my lips, of the thrumming of my heart, the sweat pooling in my palms and the deep low down tickle that felt like it was radiating from the pit of my stomach.

Right now, it's you, I heard him think, and as I breathed, he moved in, chasing away the rest of the space between us.

His lips met mine and his hand came up around me, pulling me closer to him. My eyes closed as I let myself fall into his embrace, fall into his kiss. I didn't know what to think, thoughts were impossible to form. All I could focus on was the soft slow movement of his lips that sent tingling electricity sparking through my veins.

He pulled away from me, still refusing to allow our faces to be more than a few inches apart, and I could feel his heated breath on my cheeks. My body was trembling. It wanted to be flush against his, and he seemed to feel it too, almost as if we were magnets that wanted to be stuck together. We had to restrain ourselves in order to keep any amount of distance between us but, like magnets, the closer we got to one another, the harder it was to resist. He neared again, his head tilting faintly and my eyes fluttered shut as I waited to feel his lips against mine again.

Then there was the soft thud of footsteps and the murmured sound of voices and Brant and I jolted away from one another just before Charlie and the boys made it to the end of the stairs. I could tell my face was flushed red as they came around the corner but no one seemed to notice. Brant was much better at appearing calm and casual. He and I watched as the three of them continued their conversation. Well, mostly it was Charlie and Jason talking as Skyler was currently stuffing his face with what appeared to be a peanut butter and banana sandwich.

"It's not my fault he liked mine better," Charlie said.

"Oh you cheat," Jason replied. They both laughed.

"Oh, hey, Ivy, we should probably get going though, it's getting late." Charlie said.

I pulled my cell phone out of my pocket and noticed that it was after eleven thirty already.

"Oh yeah," I turned to Brant, "Sorry, we really do need to get going."

"It's alright, I'll walk you out."

Brant walked us to my car. He didn't try to kiss me again, but he did grab my hand and gave it a squeeze. Such a simple action but it made my heart race all the same. It was beating loudly in my chest, and as I got in the driver's seat, I gave him one last glance before backing out of his driveway. His blue eyes shined through the dark, the sight of them sending shivers down my spine.

20

The Pieces You Didn't Leave Behind

I was still buzzing with excitement when I walked through my front door. My mind was tingling with anticipation as I thought over the possibilities for what would come next for Brant and me. I felt warm, my cheeks were flushed. The memory of him kissing me repeated itself over and over in my mind, like a looped tape that keeps replaying the best part of your favorite song. I could almost still feel his heated breath warming my face; almost still taste the sweetness of his lips and the smoky undertone of their flavor. Or smell his cologne, a combination of scorched wood and fresh rain. I didn't think anything could bring me down from my passion induced high.

Then I saw her. Sitting on the sofa in the living room, her blonde hair pulled up into a messy bun, mascara running down her cheeks, and a white tissue clamped tightly in her hand. Mom was crying. The smile vanished from my face. The happiness that

I had been floating on disappeared and I felt as if a chain had been wrapped around my heart dragging it down to the pit of my stomach. I knew in an instant that she had found out about my father. I didn't need to read her mind, it was glaringly obvious. She turned to look at me and as her eyes locked on mine, I saw a look of horror overcome her features. Quickly she wiped her face trying to brush away the smeared makeup and falling tears. I was at her side in seconds pulling her into a hug.

She held me tight and sobbed into my shoulder without saying a word. It felt strange to comfort her. She was my mom; she was always the one who was there for me. She was the one who held me, not the other way around. But that was exactly what was happening, and it was a little disorienting to have the roles reversed.

I felt my own eyes begin to tear up and wetness started to roll down my face. This was what I'd feared since hearing my father's thoughts at dinner that night. This is what I'd wished she wouldn't have to go through. My father's affair hurt me as his daughter, but it didn't compare to the utter devastating heartbreak I knew my mom was experiencing.

After a short while, her sobbing began to ebb and she pulled away from me. I sat down next to her on the couch and this time she pulled me to her and kissed me on the forehead. She sighed as she pulled herself together then looked down at me with a sad expression.

"Ivy, honey, there's something we need to talk

about."

I noticed the few boxes that were scatted throughout the living room. "He's moving out?" I asked but I knew the answer.

She nodded then thought, *she probably knows a lot more than you think.*

"Are you getting a divorce?"

Her lips thinned. *Yes,* "I'm not sure, sweetie. Right now we just need some time apart."

I nodded.

"Are you okay?"

"I think so," I said. It was a strange question and at the moment I wasn't sure if I knew the answer. "Are you?"

For a second she looked like she was going to start crying again, then she nodded. "Yes, yeah, I'm going to be fine."

"I love you, Mom," I said and she smiled, pulling me into a hug again.

After talking with my mom, I went up to bed. It was late and I'd had a long day. Sleep came easy. Waking the next morning, however, came with an abrupt shaking of my bed. I was jostled from my slumber by the feeling of small hands on my arm tugging at my skin. In the back of my mind there was the mumbled drone of raised voices. Slowly my eyes opened and I was met with the image of huge dark blue orbs staring at me with their watery depths. Blonde hair fell into Sadie's face.

"Mom and Dad are fighting again," she said, once she realized that I was awake. *I'm scared,* I heard her think and I scooted over in bed so she could crawl in beside me.

Glancing at my alarm clock, I saw that it was six a.m., far too early for a Sunday. Sadie snuggled into my form as the sound of breaking glass could be heard from downstairs and I tightened my grip around her. Their voices were angry and, while muffled by distance and thin walls, it was still possible to catch the pain and anger that lied within them.

"Ivy?"

"Yeah?"

"Do Mom and Dad hate each other now?" Her question was tragic for the simple fact that she had to ask it.

"No... they're just having a fight."

"Are they gonna make up?"

I decided to be honest. "I don't know," I said and she simply nodded. She may have only been eight but she was old enough to understand what was going on. "We're gonna be fine though, no matter what, okay?"

I felt her nod and I did my best to try and fall back to sleep. Before I drifted off again, I realized that she would need me. Mom would need me. I had to be there for them, had to do whatever it took. I still loved my dad but Mom and Sadie were the ones that were hurt here, especially Sadie. She didn't deserve any of this, certainly didn't ask for any of it. After Dad left, Mom would need to work more, she'd be upset, depressed, and Sadie would suffer. I knew then that I needed to step up and be there for her. I needed to look after my little sister.

It was noon by the time I got up. When I woke, I
found that Sadie had already left my room. As I made
my way down the stairs, I took note that the yelling
that had in part woken me that morning was over.
There was a dent in the living room wall revealing
the white plaster behind the beige paint, and I
noticed that the ornate stained glass vase that, as of
yesterday, had held flowers was now missing. I
turned away from the living room and made my way
into the kitchen. It was empty. On the fridge was a
note. Mom would often leave me notes on the fridge
although usually it would be after school when I
would find them.

After reading it, I learned that Mom had gone to
the grocery store with Sadie. She had a small list of
chores for me to do and one line that read, '*your
father won't be home tonight, if you need him for
anything you can call his cell*'.

I finished everything on her list and then some. I
got all the laundry caught up that I knew she'd been
falling behind on. I did the dishes and vacuumed the
living room. My room was cleaned and Sadie's toys
picked up. By the time I was done, I was feeling
exhausted. I took a break, sitting down in the living
room. I was about to turn on the TV when I reached
for the remote and noticed that the picture of Dad,
Sadie and I that once sat on the end table was
missing. Looking around the room, I saw that a
number of frames which once stood on the mantle of

the fireplace were gone. None of Dad's jackets hung on the hook by the door; he didn't have a pair of shoes resting under the coffee table.

When I had cleaned the bathroom earlier, I noticed that his shaving kit was missing from the countertop. When I did the laundry, I hadn't washed any of his clothes. He didn't have any papers scattered across the kitchen table. He didn't have anything here. It was as if any trace that he had ever existed had been removed. I realized then that he really was gone. When that realization hit me, I felt my heart plummet into the depths of my stomach like a sinking ship. I slumped deeper into the cushions of the sofa. My limbs felt heavy, they felt weak, and I began to cry. I didn't sob, I didn't bawl or whimper. The tears simply rolled from my eyes as I sat there still as stone. Slow and steady, the wet orbs tumbled across my skin and fell from my chin splashing in my lap. He was really gone.

21

And the Dish Ran Away with the Spoon

A few hours later, I was helping Mom make dinner. She thanked me for the work I'd done around the house and did her best to appear pulled together when I knew she was falling apart. Sadie seemed complacent to play in the living room while we worked and for that I was grateful. I was worried about her.

Our conversation was casual as we cocked. Mom took the time to focus on what she was doing, possibly in an attempt to keep her mind from wandering to things that she'd rather not think about. We were making meatloaf and she used the time to show me her tricks and shortcuts. I tried to follow her lead exactly, but there was no comparison between my sloppy imitation and the precise way she measured every ingredient with nothing but her senses as a guide. I helped peel carrots and mix the bread crumbs into the meat. I was a good student as she showed me how to make meatloaf just as her mother had showed her.

While dinner was cooking, I grabbed silverware as Mom grabbed plates and we went about setting the table. I followed her as she set the plates down, placing a fork and knife on either side of each one. She went back into the kitchen to grab glasses, and I placed a fork and knife on either side of the last plate at the table. Then I froze. There was a problem. I still had one set of silverware left in my hands. I'd grabbed four sets; she'd only grabbed three plates. I looked at the empty space at the table and suddenly the fork and knife that I held in my hand felt cold as ice. So cold that they burned and I nearly dropped them to clatter on the floor. Mom had always set a place for Dad, even when she knew he wouldn't be home for dinner. The difference that night was that it wasn't just dinner that he wouldn't be coming home for; he simply wouldn't be coming home.

After sitting down at the table, I watched Sadie enter the room. Her sight closed in on the table like a focusing lens, and I saw her turn to look at Mom as she walked in from the kitchen. Mom's steps halted, and Sadie didn't move.

"Dad doesn't have a plate."

For a moment, Mom didn't breathe. "He's not coming to dinner tonight, honey." Mom ushered Sadie over to her seat.

"But we always get him a plate."

"Well... After dinner, I wash all the dishes that are on the table, and I figured, it's kind of silly to be washing dishes that aren't dirty, don't you think?"

"I guess," Sadie said in a tone that suggested she didn't entirely believe our mother's logic.

Once we all had food on our plates and Sadie had her meatloaf sufficiently smothered in ketchup, Mom looked to me. "Ivy, think you could be home by at least five every day this week?"

"I guess, why?"

"I'm going to be working late a few nights this week and I need someone to be home when Sadie gets off the bus."

"Sure, yeah no problem."

Sadie was in an afterschool program as Dad was never home by the time her school let out, and even though Mom didn't work every day, when she did she often wasn't home until just before five. Now neither of them would be home by then. Again I was reminded that Dad just wasn't coming home. I wondered where else I would need to step up and for how long. Would Mom be working every day now? Would she always have long hours? My brain was infested with the possibilities as if they were flies swarming on the inside of my cranium. What if Mom didn't make it home until seven or eight? Would I need to take over making dinner? Would I not see my dad as much? Would I see him more? How long would this last?

I felt like I was statue made of sandstone that was slowly crumbling, my surface being worn away by the weathering effects of my life. I worried that I wouldn't be able to handle it. I worried that I'd disintegrate into sand and be swept away by the wind, until I was nothing more than desolate particles drifting further and further apart, completely incapable of being put back together again.

My anxiety continued to grow throughout dinner. By seven, I was a knotted mess of worried thoughts, fearing the future and trying to forget the past. After we ate, as I was sitting on my sofa between my mom and Sadie, my phone rang. It startled me at first and I practically jumped at the sound of it. I pulled it from my pocket and saw that I had a text message from Brant.

'Got an idea bout our bomber, u should come over,' it read.

The idea of getting away from home for a little while was more than appealing.

"Hey, Mom..."

"Yeah?"

"Do you mind if I go over to a friend's house for a little while?"

It is a school night, but she probably needs some time with friends, this has got to be hard on her. "I guess. Are you planning on being out late?"

"No, I just... I need to get out for a bit."

"Alright then, just give me a call later so I know you're alright."

"No problem, thanks Mom." I hugged her then quickly texted Brant that I was on my way.

As I drove, I found myself fussing with the radio, twisting through channels, listening to the fuzz between stations. My body was humming in anticipation, thinking about Brant and wondering what we would do that night. The memory of our kiss still lingered in my mind but my intentions that night were innocent. I thought maybe we'd play cards again, or watch a movie. I needed someone to chill with, to relax with. I was feeling stressed out and needed something to get my mind off things. At home, everything was collapsing, like a skyscraper imploding to make space for something new, whereas things with Brant and I were building. There was a sense of hope with us, a new beginning.

Again I let myself in through the sliding glass door, feeling oddly comfortable in his home as I'd only been there a few times. I made my way down the basement steps, calling his name as I went. When I rounded the corner, I saw him there flipping through channels on the TV. He smiled at me and turned the TV off.

"Hey," he said.

I smiled. "How's it going?" I asked taking a seat next to him.

"Great, actually. I've had some ideas about how to find this guy and I was thinking we could talk about our game plan."

My smile faded a little. He had said in his text that he wanted to talk about the bomber, but I was kind of hoping that he was just using that as an excuse to get me to come over. I needed a break from the bomber, a break from my family, a break from my life if I could help it.

"Actually, I was kind of hoping that we could just hit pause for a little while on the whole school exploding thing. Can we just forget about it for a few days?"

Forget about it? "Ivy, we've only got like two weeks left."

"Yeah, I know. I just don't want to deal with it right now."

Brant's left eyebrow lifted in confusion, bending the tiny heart-shaped birthmark above it out of shape. *You don't want to deal with knowing that someone wants to kill us all?*

"No I don't," I snapped, "Can't you just be on my side right now and forget about the bomber?" I found myself agitated with him, and shifted uncomfortably in my seat. I knew I shouldn't be taking my anger out on him, he didn't know, but I couldn't help it.

"Whoa, hey I didn't even say it out loud, sorry... I know you've had some hard stuff going on..." *I just don't know how you could forget about something like this.*

I bit my lip, but it didn't help. The words kept spilling out. "You know? What do you know? You don't know what it's like to hear them... I know you've been through some hard stuff too, Brant, but you don't know what it's like to be able to listen in on what people are thinking. To have their voices push their way into your mind. I know things that I'm not supposed to know."

He sighed. "Yeah, but you know how to turn it off, how to keep them out… And, you're right we've been relying on your ability a lot lately to figure this stuff out, but we're the only ones who can do something about this." He was trying to be reassuring, but nothing could reassure me then.

I shook my head. "You mean *I'm* the only one who can do something about this. I'm not a hero, Brant, I'm just me… I'm seventeen, this shouldn't be all on me."

"It's not… I know you think you can't do this Ivy, that *we* can't, but we can. Trust me, and once we find this guy then that's it. It's over."

I felt the frustration boiling in my veins and I shook my head. "No," I practically shouted. I felt my throat start to constrict and the tears start to pool into my eyes. "It's not *over* then," I sighed and stood up feeling the need to pace. My voice started to grow in volume, and my tone shook with emotion. "It's not over, it's *never* over. I won't ever stop hearing voices. They're always going to be there. I'm always going to hear things that no one ever meant for me to hear… hear their secrets, their private thoughts, hear the things that were never meant for my ears. Do you think I want to be like this? That I'm having *fun* searching for this psycho…"

Of course not, Brant thought but I didn't slow down to give him time to speak.

"That I want to know about my Dad cheating on my Mom, that I saw their divorce coming miles away? That *her* name is Liz and that he's been sneaking around for weeks?"

Brant stood up, suddenly understanding what had me so worked up.

My voice was starting to crack. "I didn't ask to be like this. I didn't want this."

He moved to stand inches before me, waiting for me to give him the chance to comfort me. Tears were threatening to spill, but I wasn't ready to stop and cry yet.

"It's never gonna stop, Brant."

His hands were on my arms, offering a warm solid embrace.

"I'm always going to be like this, it's always..."

His lips were on mine, smothering my words. Suddenly all my thoughts disappeared and I fell into him. He pulled me tight against him, and as his hands moved to slide up my back, mine were tangling in his hair. His lips were soft but his kiss was firm and passionate. The way our lips danced together was hungry and felt wild with longing, as if we could never be close enough. His hands rubbed at my back, fingers kneading my flesh, while mine gently pulled at his hair. Brant wasn't cautious or nervous. He was confident and kissed me deeper than anyone ever had before.

Finally our lips parted but he still held me close, held me tight. My breath was heavy and labored, my nerves were buzzing and my skin was alive with electricity. My fingers were still twisted in his hair unwilling to let go, but he seemed to have the same urge to hold me as his hands were slowly sliding back

and forth across my back. I felt the wetness of my
tears on my cheeks and they tingled under the
hotness of his breath. I wasn't crying though. The
overwhelming urge to sob had ceased. It was replaced
by the insistent need to feel him.

I brought my lips back up to his, soft at first then
I dove back into the way he was making me feel. His
hands traveled down to the hem of my shirt and
slowly one hand trailed up under the back of my top.
The other hung there loosely with his thumb looped
in the waistband of my jeans. I felt his rough,
calloused palm on my fevered skin; his touch, the
feeling of his skin on mine, sent shivers through me.
He backed me up then, stepping slowly and moving
me with him until he had me firmly pushed up
against the wall. His hand twisted around, sliding
across my back and moved to linger on the waist line
of my jeans. The tips of his fingers lightly grazed the
skin of my belly.

God, do I want you.

That moment with my back against the wall and
his body pressed up against mine, all I could think
was that I wanted more of him, and it was then that
he pulled away. Our lips parted, causing my eyes to
snap open. His forehead was pressed against mine
but the rest of my body was left absent of his touch.
His hands left my waist and his body pulled away
from me. He pressed his palms flat against the wall
on either side of my head and his blue eyes shone
down at me appearing dark as the midnight sky. His
expression reminded me of when I first started

hearing the voices and he sat down beside me in Psych, appearing to be fighting the cravings of nicotine withdrawal.

He was breathing heavy. "Maybe we should slow down a bit here," he said.

My brain was too muddled to comprehend his words at first. It wasn't until he pushed back from the wall and stepped away from me that I understood them. My legs felt too weak to work and I stood there leaning against the wall as I watched him stalk toward the bed. I felt frazzled. It was like I'd been making my way up the high dive ladder, heart pounding with fear and excitement in every step that brought me closer to the top. It felt like I had walked out all the way to the edge of the diving board to look out to the pool below only to be stopped there. He backed away from me, leaving me standing ten feet in the air lightly bouncing on the edge of the board with anticipation steaming in my veins. I wanted to jump, wanted to dive in, but it was like I suddenly realized that the pool below had no water in it.

I took a deep breath and finally found my legs to be solid as I took a step toward him. Staring at his back, I watched his shoulders rise and fall as he took a deep breath then he ran a hand through his hair. Slowly he turned around to face me.

"Is something wrong?" I asked, feeling self-conscious and unsure of myself.

His eyes went wide, "No, no nothing's wrong I just... I don't want to get... carried away."

I sighed, "Getting carried away doesn't sound so

bad right now."

He smiled that self-assured grin of his. *Don't tempt me.* His grin slowly vanished. "Your parents are getting a divorce?"

My eyes fluttered to the ground and I shifted uncomfortably from one foot to the other. Brant noticed my unease and went over to sit on the edge of the bed. He gestured for me to sit beside him and I did.

"Yeah," I said as I sat down, "Mom told me last night that he was moving out."

"Sorry, that can't be easy."

"You know, I didn't think it would be as hard as it is... I was fine, really... then today, I just... wasn't."

He brought a hand up to my back then and rubbed in slow circles to comfort me. I leaned against him, resting my head on his shoulder, and it felt like the most natural position in the world to be in.

"I feel better now though," I confessed. "It all seems a little easier when I'm around you."

Slowly I raised my head off his shoulder and looked up at him. His eyes rocked back and forth as if he were trying to read my mind. There were thoughts passing through his head, all of them like mist floating in and out and mixing together. He was wondering what I thought of him, what I wanted from him. He thought that I was beautiful, that he wanted to kiss me, to touch me. They were these vaporous, intangible things that, as I heard them, I wondered if they were really thoughts at all, wondered if maybe I was imagining them. His

eyelashes fluttered and that magnetic feeling
returned. I felt inescapably drawn to him.

My eyes moved up and down, bouncing between
his eyes and his lips. I felt myself leaning into him as
if I were teetering on a sharp point, letting gravity
push me over the edge. Then before I knew it, I was
kissing him again. Our movements didn't start out as
frantic and fevered as they were before. They were
slow, almost cautious. He kissed me lightly. His
fingers grazed a feather-soft touch across my arm.
My fingers twisted the hem of his t-shirt and I waited
in anticipation for what he would do next. Slowly he
brought a hand up my side. His fingers slid over my
ribs one by one, gently moving higher.

Our kiss deepened and I felt him gently pushing
me back onto the mattress. As my own brain raced, I
caught snippets of his thoughts. He seemed to be
trying to convince himself that kissing me would be
as far as this would go. He seemed to be worried that
what we had would be ruined if we moved too fast. I
was lying on his bed with the blue comforter beneath
me. We shifted and squirmed to find a more
comfortable position and then he was directly above
me and my knee was bent as my leg curled over one
of his.

He pulled away for a short moment to take a
breath. That was when I heard him, in his thoughts,
as he stared down at me he resigned to his feelings.
Rationality lost out over a mix of hormones and
desire. He already knew that he wouldn't stop this, it
would go as far as I'd let him take it. Then the

question was, how far was I going to let it go? Being unable to focus on anything other than the feel of his lips, the feel of his fingers slowly sliding up beneath my shirt, his hard body flush with mine, this was not an ideal time to weigh the options sensibly.

My hands were currently running up his back, underneath his shirt, finding the fabric inhibiting my intentions. I grabbed the offending material, tugging it upward until I reached his arms and could go no further. Brant pulled away from me and pulled his shirt off, casting it aside. It was then that I made my decision. A decision that was truly made on desire and lust and nothing of substance, but it was what it was. I didn't take the time to think about it with a level head because it had snuck up on me and I was left to make that decision in a vulnerable place while we lay half-naked in his bed.

We fumbled and twisted as we tried to move without breaking the contact between our lips. He was pulling at the hem of my shirt as my nails lightly scraped along his back. He lifted my top up and I raised my arms above my head and arched my back off the mattress to give him better access. I felt the chill of the air on my skin as my shirt went flying across the room. For a moment, my breath hitched in my throat, I felt nervous and exposed. Then Brant chased my nerves away with a fiery kiss. His fingers roamed across my skin, tentatively moving from the spans of flesh that he knew well to more unfamiliar territories. Somewhere in our frenzied movements, I found myself fumbling with the buckle of his belt, felt his hands tugging at the button of my jeans. There was a collage of items being unfastened, unclasped, tugged and pulled. Skin met skin and I shivered in excitement.

His lips left mine for longer than I would have liked. I tilted my head back and closed my eyes as my mind finally had a moment to catch up with all the thoughts that our passionate moment had chased away. Thoughts raced through my mind, thoughts of what I was about to do, that this was really going to happen. In the back of my mind, I heard Brant moving around, there was a ruffling of sounds, ripping of paper. There was shifting and sliding and the feeling of chilly air across my entire body. When I opened my eyes Brant, was looking down at me again. Our eyes met and for a short moment, neither of us moved. He stared deep into my eyes, a loving and caring bottomless gaze. Then he kissed me again.

22

The World Keeps Spinning Round

Butterfly kisses had trailed down my neck. Part memory, part dream, the images fluttered in my mind. Soft lips, a slow sway, whispered gasps and murmured sighs. I woke with the flashes of memory drifting through my mind. I woke to the feeling of a soft cotton comforter against my skin and a warm body at my side. My feet kicked, finding the sheets pushed to the end of the bed, their fabric just grazing my toes, and my eyes opened to see spiraling waves of blue staring back at me.

"Hey," Brant said, his voice low and raspy.

I smiled as I stretched. "Hey." My voice was soft and a little squeaky.

"You're cute when you sleep."

I smiled, feeling my cheeks flush with embarrassment. "What time is it anyway?"

Brant rolled over to look at the large digital numbers on an old alarm clock that sat on the table across the room. I looked in the same direction. They read 12:00. I sat up suddenly, surprised at how late it was.

"I have to go," I said as I started searching for my clothes. I dug around for the scattered pieces of my wardrobe and dressed in haste. "I'm sorry; I didn't realize how late it was." When I finally looked back to Brant, he was up as well and had thrown his jeans on. My eyes raked up his shirtless form then settled on his eyes.

"It's okay," he said. "I understand."

Brant walked over to me as I pulled my shirt in place and slid on my shoes. I looked up to him to find him watching my every move. I slowed down and took a breath. He smiled at me then leaned in for a short kiss.

I snuck into the house. The lights were out and it was quiet as I tiptoed through the front door. Mom and Sadie had already gone to bed. I just hoped that she hadn't waited up for me. I didn't have any missed phone calls or texts, but that didn't mean that my mom wasn't upset with me. As quietly as I could, I closed the door behind me and made my way up the stairs.

I didn't think much about what had happened between Brant and me as I walked into my bedroom and dressed for bed. I felt sore, felt tired, but my brain was focused on falling asleep so that I could wake up easily for school.

The next day started out like any other. I got up, got dressed, drove to school. But one thing was different-me. On my drive to school, I started to wonder if I was happy about the decisions I'd made. During my short time in the car, I thought about my previous night with Brant. I thought about how upset I had been about my dad, about my abilities, and the weight that I felt was resting on my shoulders. I had been raw with emotion, I had been needy, and I sought comfort in him. I knew that I cared about him, but we'd taken this huge step and we weren't even dating. We hadn't proclaimed our undying love to one another or even so much as declared ourselves to be in a relationship. I had wanted to sleep with him, but in that moment I wondered if I had been wrong to act on want alone.

I hadn't thought it through and now there was no going back. Last night had been, well honestly, it had been incredible but I had no idea if it was worth it. I hadn't planned for things to go as far as they did that night. When it came down to it I didn't have time to think before I acted. I got caught up in my emotions, got caught up in him, and all rational thought had gone out the window. Like an amusement park ride gone rogue everything quickly spun out of control.

I grew nervous. I felt so unsure of myself, worried that I had made a mistake. I did honestly believe that Brant cared for me. I didn't think he'd play me or try and hurt me, but what it came down to was that I didn't really know. I had no idea where we were headed. I had no reassurance that I wasn't going to end up hurt. All I could do was wait and see as I'd already made my choices. The day before, all I had was hope for what was to come between Brant and I, and that hope wasn't gone. But there was a new sense of fear and uncertainty that now accompanied it.

When I got to school, I saw Brant, Jason and Skyler all hovering in their usual shadowed spot on the side of the building. The darkness of the shadows seemed deeper with the overcast sky above, and their faces were impossible to read. Clouds, the color of ash and soot, hung in the air, a screen of haze that blocked out the blue sky. I glanced at the guys and wondered if Brant was talking about me. I wondered if he was telling them every detail about our night together. I didn't think he would. I wanted to believe that what we had shared was special and that he wouldn't betray my trust like that. In truth, though, I simply didn't know. As my paranoia ate away at me, I was about to listen in on their thoughts, but then Charlie walked up to me.

"Hey," she called and my head jerked to face her.

"Hey," I responded with surprise in my voice. She had startled me. I gave Brant and his friends one last glance and saw that Brant was making his way toward us, then I turned back to Charlie. "How's it going?"

"Good, how about you? Did the rest of your weekend go well?" I thought about my parents, Mom crying, one plate missing from the dining room table, then I thought about Brant and I and felt a shiver run through me.

"Um, fine. Yeah, it was alright. How about you?"

Charlie was about to respond, but then Brant was right beside us.

"What was just alright?" he asked.

"What? Nothing."

He and I stared at one another for a moment in awkward silence.

"My weekend was good," Charlie said bringing my mind back to reality. Her eyes bounced between Brant and I. "So, anyway," Charlie continued. "I'm hoping the computers will be back up today, you guys wanna meet me at lunch?"

It took a moment to register what she had asked me. "What, um yeah, yeah we'll meet you there."

"Okay, good." She paused, her eyes again floating back and forth between us. "Is everything okay with you two?"

I don't know, Brant thought.

"Yep," I said quickly, "everything's peachy." A fake smile graced my face.

The bell rang and I shuffled off to class without saying goodbye to either of them. I could feel both Brant and Charlie staring holes into the back of my head as I walked away. I knew I was acting oddly, I just didn't know how I was supposed to be. Everything had changed between Brant and I, and I didn't know how to handle it. Were we supposed to go on like nothing had happened, were we supposed to be all over one another, should I have kissed him goodbye? I didn't know what any of it meant. Was it just a one night fling or did this mean something to him? All I knew was that it meant everything to me. I needed to know what he thought, how he felt.

I slowed my step and tried to listen in on Brant's thoughts without turning around. If last night meant nothing to him, I couldn't let him see the pained look on my face. I heard various voices shift through my mind, but I found that it was hard to focus on Brant when I wasn't looking at him. Finally, after some fumbling with my ability, I locked in on him.

I just wish I knew what she was thinking, I heard.

Before I could hear anything else, though, there was a hand on my arm distracting me.

"Hey," Charlie said and I slowed down to face her. "What's wrong?"

I stopped walking all together. "Nothing, really..."

"No, it's not nothing, come on. Talk to me."

"We don't have time right now, I have to get to class."

Students walked by on either side of us, some bumping into us as they pushed their way toward the door.

"You have Math first hour, yeah? Sumner or Berger?" Charlie asked.

"Sumner."

"Good, because he has a sub today and I have study hall first hour."

Her offer was tempting, but I didn't need to land in anymore trouble. "I can't skip class."

"Yes you can. Not something I world normally

condone, but you're upset and half the time subs never take attendance anyway."

"What if he does? My mom would kill me if I got a Saturday detention."

"Then I promise to hack into the school computer system and change your absent mark to a present one."

I thought over her suggestion. I did need to talk to someone and I couldn't talk to Brant. I finally decided to go with her and nodded in agreement.

Charlie and I sat down in the study hall room at an open table. The air was stale and dry smelling musty like the attic of my house. It reminded me of old dusty books forgotten and left beneath a bed or shut away in a closet somewhere, and it was quiet with only a low murmur of whispered voices to fill the space. Around us there were a number of other tables, some with large groups of people at them working on projects, others with small groups of people working silently by themselves. Charlie and I had a table to ourselves, and for that I was grateful.

For a short while, as I sat across from her, I was silent. "So... do you really know how to hack into the school computer system?" I asked.

Charlie shrugged. "Yeah, I do."

"Do you do that often? Hack in, get yourself out of detentions, change grades."

"No, I've never actually done it. I guess I only ever hacked into it in the first place to see if I could."

"Why don't you?"

"It's just not my thing, I guess. I like to play by

the rules... for the most part at least. But that's beside the point. We're supposed to be here to talk about you."

I sighed. "Right, me."

"Yeah, you... so what's up with the weirdness? You and Brant were being all twitchy around each other this morning. Did something happen with you guys?"

"Yeah... something happened." I was silent then.

Charlie looked on at me for a few moments, waiting for me to speak again. "Okay... Ivy, you're the one that can read minds here not me, so if you want to talk to me about this, you're going to have to actually tell me what happened."

I sighed. "Last night, I went over to Brant's house... I was upset... my, um, my parents are getting a divorce."

"I'm sorry," Charlie said, looking truly sincere.

"It's okay, I'm... dealing."

"So, did he say something... insulting?"

I sighed. "No, he was... comforting, he was just... he was too comforting."

How could someone be too comforting? Charlie thought, then I saw the look of confusion on her face transform. Her eyes grew wide and she took a sharp intake of breath. "Oh," she said. I didn't need to listen in on her thoughts to know that she knew what I meant. "Have you ever, *you know*, before?"

I felt my cheeks blush and I couldn't look at her. Instead, I focused intently on my fingernails. "No, he was... he was the first." When my eyes met hers again, she offered me a comforting smile.

"You guys aren't dating are you?"

"No... last night," I found my voice at the lowest audible whisper, "it just happened."

She paused for a moment. "Did he... try... did you not want to?"

"It's not like that. We both wanted to, but now... I just don't know what to do now. I don't know what any of it meant to him. Like you said, we aren't dating... I'm worried that I made a mistake."

"Have you talked to him about it?"

I felt my skin redden with embarrassment once again at the thought of talking to him, "No... I don't know how. I'm too worried to find out that he doesn't really feel the same way about me."

"How *do* you feel about him?"

Her question took me a little off guard. I hadn't taken much time to put my feelings for Brant into words. I knew I liked him, that I cared about him. I didn't think I loved him. I'm not sure at that point I really knew what being in love felt like, as I'd never been in love before. What I did know was that I felt safe with Brant. I felt like I could talk to him, tell him anything. I felt like he would look after me, like he'd keep my secrets safe. I knew he made my heart beat faster. I knew that I wanted to be around him every second I could manage.

In that moment, I thought two things. First I wondered if maybe I did love him. I did feel for him in a way that I had never felt before. The second was that I trusted Brant and I realized that I had been over-thinking the entire situation. Not to say that the magnitude of what had happened between us was lessened, just that I was spending too much energy worrying about it. Instead of being paranoid about the worst possible outcome coming true, I needed to talk to Brant and find out where we stood with one another.

I looked for Brant after leaving the study hall room. I had about twenty minutes before second hour started. Brant should have still been in class, but I hoped that he had snuck out for a smoke. When I stepped out onto the courtyard, however, my eyes focused on someone else. Tiana sat at her usual table, but she sat there alone. No Christy, no Eliza, just Ti. It wasn't lunch, but for a moment I thought about how, if Christy had a Student Council meeting and if Eliza and Damon were to go off campus for lunch, Ti would be sitting there eating alone.

Suddenly, I realized something; I realized how my spending time with Brant had made her feel. She and I had always stuck together, always had each other's backs. She had been there for me when Christy showed up with Chase at Eliza's, we had each other to eat with every day at lunch when the others were elsewhere. She had confided in me about her seeing Brant when she felt like she couldn't tell anyone else. I hadn't intended to, but I had betrayed her.

Despite how she treated Brant, she had cared about him, maybe cared the same way that I did now. Even though she had been wrong about Brant and I seeing each other when she accused us of it, even though that hadn't been my secret then, I had still been hiding something from her. Looking at her sitting alone at that table, I realized how much my actions had isolated her. For the first time, neither one of us had backed the other up and it killed something important in our friendship.

I walked toward her and thought about how I would feel if I showed up at school tomorrow to find Brant giving some girl a ride to class, thought about how even if we stopped hanging out that it would hurt to see him talking with someone else. Tiana was reading and taking notes from her Physics book, but looked up to me as I neared. I met her eyes and she glared at me silently as I sat down before her.

"I wanted to say I'm sorry," I said.

She was silent.

"I never mean to hurt you."

Yeah, well you did, I heard her think, but she said nothing.

"I know you feel betrayed, I know I wasn't there for you, and I'm sorry."

She looked away from me, her eyes searching into the distance. I sighed and stood from the table. I hadn't expected her to accept my apology. I hadn't expected anything really. I had just felt the need to tell her that I knew I'd hurt her. I felt her eyes turn back toward me as I began to walk away.

It was my fault too, she thought, and for a moment I paused. *I didn't tell you everything, you didn't know how I felt about him.* "Ivy, wait..." she said.

I turned around.

"Thank you," she said. Then after a long pause, "I'm sorry too."

I nodded and felt a sense of resolve between us. Maybe not enough for us to ever be friends like we were, but enough to feel the tension that had been there melt away. I smiled at her and walked back inside.

It was lunch when I saw Brant next. I ran into him in the hallway on my way to the library. At first I felt my nerves winding and twisting together like vines working their way up a trellis. Then I took a deep breath and confronted him. I walked across the hall. He noticed me as I got close and slowed down. I took note that he seemed as nervous as I was.

Ivy, he thought as he spotted me, the sound of his inner voice holding excitement and worry all within the short two syllables of my name.

"Hey," I said, "I think maybe we should talk."

His eyes darkened on my words and silently he nodded. I smiled softly then turned away from him without another word. He followed me as I weaved past the other students in the hall and went out onto the common. We sat down at our usual table. For a moment we were both silent. I felt nervous and twitchy and began fidgeting with my fingernails. Then finally my eyes met his.

"Last night... When we..." I paused. My voice was caught, trapped by my nerves. "God, I don't know how to say this."

The muscles in Brant's jaw twitched. "Look,

forget it, you were upset... if it didn't mean anything to you, don't worry about it. Just cold comfort, yeah?"

After hearing those words, the feeling that came over me was that of being on some speedy snaking and convulsing carnival ride after eating nothing but fried and sugary food.

I can deal, he thought.

"Is that how you feel? Did it not mean anything to you?" Every word was shaky, each sentence a step closer to bringing me to tears. My muscles tightened and I practically held my breath in anticipation for his response.

God no, he thought. "I'm just saying, it doesn't have to mean anything, not if you don't want it to."

"Do *you* want it to? God, Brant, I am tired of defensiveness and mixed signals." I took a breath and summoned the last of the courage I had. "I like you, I have feelings for you, and last night was... it meant something to me. I just don't know if it meant anything to you." My eyes were pleading with him, pleading for an answer no matter what it was. I needed to know, even if his answer wasn't what I wanted it to be.

"It meant something to me too, it meant a lot. I thought... it was just this morning you seemed... I thought you regretted it."

I shook my head, "I don't regret it, I wanted to, I just... what does it mean, what does that mean for us now?"

Brant smiled at me. *It means I like you too, Ivy, more than a lot.* He was leaning across the table. The skinny slab of stone between us was covered quickly as Brant reached a hand out to stroke my cheek. Then he kissed me. I leaned into him and laughed into the awkward angle of it all. I didn't care that we were out on the common and that anyone could see us, didn't care that people would stare, that they would talk. I wasn't ashamed of him. He sat back down after that with a smile on his face.

"So..." I began, but my words were cut off by a voice over the loud speaker.

'Attention ALH students, the assembly that was scheduled for the twenty-fifth has been moved to this Friday. Please be prepared to meet in the gym during first hour in your spirit wear. Again the assembly will no longer be the Monday after next, it will be this Friday. All students are required to attend in school colors. Thank you."

This Friday was the fifteenth. The assembly would be for *The Play in the Park*. I remembered Christy talking to her mom on the phone about it.

"School assembly, fun," I said sarcastically.

Brant, however, didn't seem to hear me. His eyes were staring off into the distance but looking at nothing in particular. His mind was racing, mulling something over. I could almost picture his thoughts churning like cogs in a machine.

Monday after next, that's it, Brant thought.

I looked at him confused. "What?"

"The Monday after next, that's when everything's supposed to go down, yeah?"

The bomber's thoughts rang through my mind, *a*

month from now they'll all be dead, and the Monday after next would be that day. The same day we were supposed to have had an assembly.

"You think whoever's been planning this chose that Monday because of the assembly?"

"Think about it, it makes perfect sense. The whole school together at the same time in the same place, if he wants to kill us all he'll need us all together."

"Now that the assembly is moved you don't think he'll move his plans up too, do you?"

"I'm thinking he'll have to. We just had our time to find him cut in half."

It made sense, perfect sense, and that frightened me. Now instead of having two weeks to figure out who wanted us all dead, we had until Friday. As the day was already half way over and the assembly was first hour on Friday, that left us with three days. We only had three days. I felt the panic set in. My heartbeat picked up and I started to worry that it wouldn't be enough time.

"We have to find Charlie," I said. "We need to figure this out now."

We raced to the library, knowing that our conversation over personal matters had taken up valuable time. The lunch hour was winding down and we couldn't afford to waste another second. Charlie spotted us right away when we walked through the glass doors. She seemed excited and as we approached, I hoped that she had gotten to the information that we so desperately needed.

"I got it," she said as we approached the desk. She

picked up a stack of papers that she had sitting on the desk and held it up with enthusiasm. "Book rentals, website searches, it's all here."

"Good," I said, "'Cause we've only got 'til Friday now."

Charlie's eyes went wide with alarm. "What, why?"

"The assembly," Brant said.

Charlie's expression lit up. I could see all the pieces come together behind her eyes. "The assembly, right... They moved it up because they had to move the date of the *Play in the Park*. Mrs. Emmeric had a note about it in her calendar. They're doing it almost a month sooner, and they'll be gathering all the students in the gym to talk to us about it. Oh God."

"Yeah, so we have to figure this out fast."

Charlie nodded in agreement. It was then, however, that the bell rang, signaling the end of the lunch hour.

"We'll have to look through all of this later though."

"You guys want to come over to my place after school?" Brant suggested.

"I can't, I have to be home for when my little sister gets there. You guys could come to my place though."

"Yeah, no problem," Charlie said and Brant nodded in agreement. As we all parted and went off toward our separate classes, I hoped that we would find what we needed quickly and easily.

23

Start Looking

After class, we met up at my house and spread out in the living room to look over the papers that Charlie had printed earlier that day. Sitting on the floor, we started with the book rental records and divvied up the pages. The lists were organized by book title, so it was our job to find people that rented multiple books. Highlighter in hand, I scrolled down the page, grateful that Charlie had at least been able to get a print up of only the books related to bombings and not the entire school library. Still, it was a tedious task. I highlighted any name I saw twice, trying to do each name in a different color. Finally I reached the last name on the last page of my section and I sighed in relief.

"How are you guys doing?" I asked setting down my papers.

"Think I've got three names here that stand out," Brant said.

"I've got about the same," Charlie agreed.

I flipped through my pages. "I probably have like four, but some of those should overlap with what you guys have too, so that's not so bad."

Brant set down his papers, finished with his share. "So what now?"

"Oh, um," Charlie started shifting through her bag and pulled out more papers, "I have a list of names here of anyone who looked up anything bomb-related on a campus computer this year." The list was at least three pages long. "Guess now we should compare."

"See who's got check marks in multiple columns," Brant said, "Oh, and we have our list of ten names from the hardware store to look at as well."

"Hopefully this narrows us down to one name," I said with a sigh.

Charlie and Brant nodded in agreement and we continued on with our research.

I guessed that it was about five-thirty when we finished. The sun had yet to set but sat low on the horizon. The living room grew darker and I had turned on the lamp that sat on the end table behind me. Names were written down, rewritten, crossed out. We compared all the lists, did our best to narrow our leads. Who was searching bombings, checking out books on them, and buying ingredients? In the end, it came down to one name, one person. It seemed too perfect to be a coincidence. But there was one problem with what we concluded, and that was the name that we narrowed it down to. It was Eric

Thompson.

I shook my head, this couldn't be right. "I don't get it. We ruled him out."

"Yeah, but you did say he gave you a weird feeling." Brant said.

"Still though, his voice wasn't the same, and he wasn't at school on Thursday when I heard the second voice." *It won't be a big enough explosion, we need more.* I heard in my head again.

"He might have lied about not being at school," Charlie suggested, "I could check the attendance records and double check... Maybe he thought you were on to him."

I began to second guess myself. "I guess, and you're right, he did give me a weird vibe."

"It's got to be him, Ivy," Brant said. "He's the only one on all three lists. No one else was researching bombs, and extensively I might add, and bought supplies for them with his mother's credit card."

I nodded, "You're right, I guess it's just blowing my mind a bit. We had him, you know."

Before anyone could say another word, the front door opened and my mom walked in. She looked frazzled from a long day at work but smiled as she saw us sitting in the living room. I said hello as she set her briefcase down and took her jacket off to hang on the coat rack. She smiled as she greeted Charlie and looked Brant up and down with a quick scanning of her eyes.

"You guys working on homework?" she asked and we were quick to agree. "Well, I won't keep you then.

If you kids get hungry, just holler, I can throw a pizza in."

"Thanks, Mom," I said as she made her way up the stairs.

We all waited until she was out of sight to begin talking again. However, before I could get a full sentence out, she reappeared on the stairs.

"Ivy, where's Sadie?"

My eyes went wide and I felt all the color drain from my face. I quickly grabbed my phone and saw how late it was. Sadie should have come home from her after-school program more than a half hour ago. I hadn't even noticed that she hadn't walked through the door. I had been too wrapped up in my own things to even realize that she was missing. As I looked back up at my mom, I knew she could read the worry on my face.

"She never came home," I said.

Mom was at the foot of the stairs in a second. She rounded the corner in one fluid motion, making her way into the kitchen and then I could hear her dialing the phone. After that, I couldn't concentrate on anything but my little sister. I focused my ability on my mom in the kitchen. She was in another room and out of sight, which made it hard to tune in to her thoughts, but I needed to know what she was thinking. I needed to know what was going on. Then finally I was able to hear her in my head.

Mom was on the phone with Sadie's school. As she listened to the woman on the other line, I found that I could hear both their voices in my head.

Charlie said something to me, but I wasn't paying her any attention. It felt like ice was flowing through my veins and my stomach was doing flips. I needed to know what was going on.

Mom was asking if Sadie had gotten on the bus to come home after her after-school program. The woman on the phone assured her that she did. Her words, however, didn't calm my mother. She was anxious and worried and growing livid with every moment that passed. She insisted that they talk to the bus driver. She knew that Sadie got on the bus, but did she get off it?

The woman on the other line shuffled around, I heard papers ruffling. Then she told my mother to wait for a moment and she put her on hold. Minutes passed by, two, five, ten, thirteen. Mom was watching the clock. Then finally there was a click on the other line and the woman's voice returned. She said that she had just gotten off the phone with the bus driver and he had told her that Sadie got off at her usual spot. Mom thanked the woman and hung up the phone, but her time talking to her had done nothing to reassure her. Mom paused for a moment, possibly frozen in shock and fear. Then she walked back out into the living room. Her eyes were distant as she looked at me.

"I don't know where she is," Mom said. "They said she got off the bus, I don't know..."

"We'll go out and look for her," Brant said and my eyes shot to him. He stood up and Charlie and I followed.

"Yeah, we can go drive around," I said and watched as my mom nodded in agreement. "And if we don't come back soon then call the police, or call them now if it makes you feel better. We'll go find her." I walked up to my mom and gave her a hug.

All Mom could do was nod as we pulled apart, and I left with Brant and Charlie. We walked outside and I noticed a chill to the air. The wind brushed by my face and sent my hair spiraling out around me. I looked down at the car keys in my hand then down to the end of the block. I could see her bus stop from here. I closed my fingers around the keys, feeling their jagged edges and hearing the muffled sound of metal clanking against metal.

"Maybe we should walk. I'm thinking we might have better luck on foot... if she just wandered off that is." The other option was that someone grabbed her and I couldn't think about that, because if that was the case then there was nothing I could do.

Brant rubbed my back, "We'll find her," he assured me, and he sounded so confident about it. It was hard not to believe him.

"Where should we start?" Charlie asked and I pointed to the end of the block.

"Her bus stop is down there."

"Seems as good a place as any," Brant said and we all started to walk down the block.

24

I Went by Myself

The sun was setting on the horizon when we started
walking. The clouds looked like glowing orange
waves rolling in and crashing against the darkening
sky. I would have thought it was a pretty sight had I
not been so preoccupied. The bus stop may have been
a logical place to start the search for my sister, but
we didn't find her there. Once we were at the corner
of Sunnyside and Parkway, we discussed splitting up,
but neither Brant nor Charlie knew what Sadie
looked like. And, as she had never met either of
them, I couldn't imagine her reacting well to a
stranger walking up to her saying that her sister and
mother were worried about her and that she needed
to go with them, unless that was what had already
happened.

We decided to stay together and walked across
Sunnyside Lane to make our way toward the park. It
seemed the most logical direction for her to walk in

as Parkway was a much busier road, one that I wouldn't have thought she'd try to cross. As we walked, my mind wandered back to Jason and the story Brant told me about his little brother. I realized then how helpless Jason must feel. Even as I walked, I didn't know if there was really anything I could do. Jason's little brother had a good chance of beating his cancer and I suppose Sadie had a good chance of me finding her, but the panic and insecurity I felt surrounding it all was eating away at me.

"Can you think of any place she might have gone? A friend's house maybe?" Charlie asked.

"I don't know, maybe. I'm sure Mom's calling all of her friends now. I just can't imagine if she went over somewhere that they wouldn't have called Mom first though."

Sadie had never done anything like this before. Never even wandered off in the supermarket or left Mom's side at the mall. The fact that this was so unlike her was the scariest part about it.

"How old is she?" Brant asked. He'd been unusually quiet since we started walking. I hadn't listened in on any of his thoughts but I could tell by the look on his face that my missing sister fiasco was bringing him back to an earlier memory, that of his mom going missing.

"She's eight," I said and both Brant and Charlie nodded. No one said another word after that for some time.

It was a few minutes later that we neared the park. A long chain link fence surrounded its limits

and tall trees broke up the landscape. I saw the
metal skeleton of a jungle gym reaching toward the
sky in the shape of a rocket ship. It cast crisscrossing
shadows onto the grass from the last of the sun's
glimmering rays. There were picnic tables and a
gazebo, a yellow plastic slide that twisted down from
a tower, and a set of seesaws. As we got closer, more
and more of the park came into view. At the far end
of it was a cement patch with two basketball hoops
that had long ago lost their nets. Just before a small
parking lot, there was a small structure that
contained bathrooms and water fountains.

I looked around for her, praying that she'd be
here. I didn't just hope or wish to find her though. I
told myself that this is where I would find her, said it
over and over in my mind so much that I started to
believe that this was where she was. But, as I looked
around for her, as I searched for her blonde hair and
purple backpack, I found nothing. The park seemed
completely empty beyond our presence, but we kept
walking. I wondered for a moment if Brant had done
the same thing with his mom so many years ago. I
wondered if he tried to convince himself that she was
coming home. I wondered for how long he held on to
that hope that one day he'd look and she'd be there
like he expected. Did he still hope? Did he still expect
to find her?

Then finally something caught my eye. I breathed
a sigh of relief and my paced picked up. Beyond the
gazebo, a view hidden from my previous vantage
point, was a swing set. The metal chain barely

moved, but it was enough that, as I got closer, I could hear its soft squeaking. Set on the ground beside the tall metal structure was Sadie's purple backpack and sitting on the swing with her back to us was my little sister. I ran to her, around the swing set, and her face looked up to me as I came around the corner. Her blonde hair had been braided in pigtails and she wore a pink and white striped shirt with a long-sleeved grey sweater. Her small hands held on to the metal chain links of the swing and there were tears in her eyes. I scooped her up and pulled her into a tight hug.

"Where the hell have you been? Mom is freaking out!" I heard the tone of anger in my voice but it was only there to mask my concern.

Slowly I pulled away from her to leave her sitting on the swing. Kneeling before her, I looked her over, checking to make sure that she was all there. In the corner of my vision, I saw Brant and Charlie hovering some distance away, but I paid them no attention. My thumb brushed away the wetness from Sadie's cheeks and I was eager to know what had upset her.

"Are you okay? What happened?"

"Nothing happened, Ivy. I just wanted to go to the park."

I shook my head, not understanding.

"Dad wouldn't take me to the park, and now he's gone so I went by myself."

I pulled her back into a hug feeling my heart break for her.

"I'm sorry Sadie," I said, "I'm really sorry... let's go home though, okay? Mom's really worried about you."

Sadie nodded at me and we both stood up. I watched as she put her backpack on and I grabbed her hand as we began to walk back towards my friends.

When we walked through the front door, I heard Mom hang up the phone and rush into the entryway. Her eyes immediately found Sadie and she grabbed her and pulled her into a hug. As she held her tight, she threatened her to never do that to her again. I let them be and walked outside with my friends. We hovered on the front step for a moment and stood in silence in the now dark night.

"I'm sorry about dragging you guys on that goose hunt," I said.

"It's no problem," Brant said, "we're just glad she's okay."

"Yeah, really, Ivy, we were glad to help," added Charlie.

Their sentiments warmed my heart and I offered up a grateful smile.

"Well, thank you," I said.

After that, I gave Charlie a hug and she left. I waved and watched as her headlights cut through the dark then disappeared around the corner. Brant and I sat down on the stoop, sitting side by side, and enjoyed the quiet of the night. I looked to him. His face was cast in dark angular shadows created by the porch light. He was hunched over with his hands folded between his legs. I sat with my hands resting lightly on my knees. We listened to the soft chirping of crickets and felt the cool breeze rush past us, but we didn't move. Didn't say a word, and I didn't need to nor need him to. Just being in his company was comfortable.

After a short moment, Brant unbraided his fingers and reached over to grab my hand. My fingers intertwined with his and I squeezed, comforted by the feel of his skin against mine. Wordlessly, he stood and I stood up beside him, keeping our hands linked. With his free hand, he brushed a stray hair out of my face then kissed me softly on the lips. After that, we said our goodbyes and I went back into the house.

Sadie was lying on the couch, her head on Mom's lap and her eyes closed. She snored lightly and Mom ran her fingers through her hair. There was a calm that came over the room. It contrasted heavily with the chaotic atmosphere that had been when Sadie was missing. Quietly, I sat down in the oversized chair that was adjacent to the couch. Mom looked to me with a grateful smile.

"I like your new friends," she said. "They seem like good kids."

I nodded in agreement.

"What was the boy's name?"

"Brant."

"Right, of course, he's the one that's not your boyfriend? He seemed to like you."

Her words were soft and observant as she looked at me, her eyes expressing the insight and wisdom that was rooted within their green orbs. You would have thought my mother had lived on this earth for a thousand years to absorb every bit of information there was about life and love just from the depths of her eyes.

I smiled. "I'm not so sure of that anymore," I said. "About him not being my boyfriend... he's a good guy."

Mom didn't say anything after that. She just smiled with that knowing look in her eyes.

25

Sneaking In

The next two days at school, we searched for Eric.
Charlie printed off a copy of his schedule and we
waited for him after every one of his classes. We
never saw him. I grew anxious. We needed to find
him, to talk to him. Not that any of us knew exactly
what to say when we found him, but we had to at
least try to change his mind. Our intentions,
however, never developed past the goal stage of our
plan as he wasn't at school on Tuesday or
Wednesday. Brant figured he was getting everything
prepared for Friday, and I had to admit that it
seemed likely. Part of me hoped that Eric had
changed his mind on his own. I didn't care whether or
not he had an epiphany or chickened out, but if he
just would have decided not to blow us all up, it
would have saved me a lot of trouble.

The time between thinking about Eric Thompson
and the looming death of all Alta Ladera High

students was spent fairly normally. Knowing that the bomber was Eric had put our minds at ease some. We never expected that we wouldn't see him again until Friday. So on Tuesday and Wednesday, the three of us would meet to hang out before classes as casually as if it were any other day. Brant and I would eat lunch together on the common and visit Charlie in the library before the bell rang. After school, I found myself talking with Charlie on the phone over homework which would usually lead into a conversation about something else-Brant, school, Eric, music, the winter formal. We talked about everything, and I found that she and I had much deeper conversations then I ever had with Christy or any of my previous friends. Being friends with Christy, Ti and Eliza had been a comfortable place to be, but I realized that I'd only felt that way because I'd never really gotten to know anyone else.

Both Tuesday and Wednesday night, I talked on the phone with Brant before I fell asleep. I'd lay in bed with the phone to my ear and my eyes half-closed as we continued to get to know one another. Both nights, I fell asleep with my phone in my hand and woke the next morning needing to dig for it beneath my blankets and pillows.

Things with family also went well those two days. Dad picked Sadie up after school on Tuesday and took her out for ice cream. Both Mom and I knew the things that had been happening couldn't be solved with frozen yogurt, but the sentiment seemed to help. Dad and I talked for some time that day after he dropped Sadie off at home. He didn't tell me anything that I didn't already know. It wasn't my fault, he still loved me. He even tried to sweeten the pot by reminding me that this meant twice the gifts for Christmas, but it came off like a bad joke. Of course he didn't know that I knew why they were getting a divorce. I just nodded in agreement and tried to enjoy the time with him. More than anything he said, the fact that he took the time to talk to me was what meant something.

Thursday morning, when Eric was again missing from school, we realized that we needed a backup plan. We couldn't count on hoping to run into him before the assembly. It was starting to look like things would be working down to the wire and my mind scrambled to figure out what to do next. Brant suggested calling in a bomb threat if all else failed. The only thing I could think to do was to talk to him and try and convince him to change his mind, but I needed to find him first.

Charlie looked up Eric's address on the school computers and immediately after class we drove to his house. We took the Lumina and I felt my nerves grow as we neared his block, which was in a slightly shadier part of town than I was used to visiting. Not that any part of Alta Ladera was all that shady, some streets were just less maintained then others. We pulled up outside a house with a lawn so overgrown, I wondered if it'd ever been cut. Next door a group of middle school kids sat on the porch eyeing us, and across the street a yellow lab had his head buried in the ground as he dug up a bone.

I took a deep breath, feeling nervous. Charlie and I glanced at one another and then we got out of the car. Brant, who'd been sitting in the backseat, followed. We walked up the steps and stood on the stoop. I knocked on the door. There were no lights on in the house and no car in the driveway. It appeared as if no one was home. I couldn't give up yet though. I rang the doorbell and held my breath in anticipation. No one came to the door. Beside me Brant had his hands up to block the sun as he peeked into the window.

"I don't think anyone's home," he said.

"Now what do we do?" I asked.

"I picked up a few other things from the library today, just in case we didn't find him," Charlie said.

I was about to ask her what they were, but it was then that I noticed Brant was no longer peeking in through the window. I looked over just in time to see him vanish around the corner of the house. Charlie and I glanced at one another then we both followed after him. We picked up our pace as we rounded the corner to see Brant already disappearing behind the house.

The backyard was fenced in by rusting chain-link, but the gate didn't have a lock. Charlie and I walked through the gate and saw Brant holding open a worn screen door and twisting the knob of the back door.

"Wait," I said.

Brant stopped. "What?"

"We can't break in."

Brant twisted the knob and let the door swing open. "It's not a B and E if the door's unlocked." He stepped inside and, cautiously, Charlie and I followed.

"How'd you know it would be unlocked?" Charlie asked.

"I didn't, just thought it was worth a shot. My dad forgets to lock the back door all the time."

Brant was peering around corners and quickly eyeing up every room he entered. Charlie and I followed him through Eric's kitchen, then the living room which smelled like coffee grounds and wilting flowers. His parents seemed to have an accumulation of secondhand furniture and flea market finds as nothing matched. They also weren't very tidy as everything was covered in a fine layer of dust. Brant peered into the dining room and then we all walked up stairs.

"What are we doing here?" I asked. "I mean, it's obvious Eric isn't home."

"Eric might not be, but this bomb he's been building has to be somewhere."

We reached the top of the stairs. Brant started pushing open doors. The first was a bathroom we passed by, the next the master bedroom. Finally we found Eric's room and Charlie and I followed Brant inside. From the second Brant pushed the door open and the smell of sweaty gym socks and stale potato chips assaulted my senses, it was obvious that this room belonged to a teenage boy. The floor was a mess with discarded clothes; the desk was cluttered with papers. The bed was unmade with its navy comforter lumped half on the floor. The curtains were pulled shut, and the walls were lined with band posters that appeared to have more Satanic references then musical ones.

"No bomb," I said, eyeing up one of the posters. It hung crooked on the wall, held up by thumb tacks. A zombie stood center stage, complete with green skin and dripping gore, but said zombie was also a woman and overtly sexualized with heaving breasts and ripped clothes. It was a disgusting mix of horror and soft-core porn.

"Good band," Brant said as he walked up behind me.

My eyebrows lifted. "Ew."

"Guys, come check this out," Charlie said.

Brant and I spun around to see her standing before Eric's desk, sifting through the papers that were scattered there.

"He's definitely our guy, look at this."

Looking over the papers, I saw that Eric had researched how to build bombs. One sheet held the pros and cons of pipe bombs; another had doodles of mushroom clouds and scribbled skeletons. It had my stomach flipping, just seeing all of that written in his handwriting. For a moment, it was hard to believe that the boy who had drawn them was the same one we used to call 'Teddy Bear Thompson'.

"So where's the bomb then?" Brant asked.

"Basement?" I suggested and he nodded.

We left Eric's room and made our way to the

kitchen then down the basement steps. The light in the stairwell was burnt out and I gripped the metal railing tight as I moved down the stairs into the musty, cold dark.

"Guys?" Charlie asked, "What are we gonna do when we find it?"

Brant thought for a moment. "Take it apart if we can. Call the police, we could say Eric showed it to us."

"You don't think they'll think we helped him build it, do you?" I asked.

"I think if we turned him in, they'd let us off the hook."

We reached the bottom of the stairs and stood in the dark while Brant fished for a string to pull and turn on a light. It was absolutely pitch black, so dark that I couldn't distinguish between closing my eyes and opening them. Then I heard the sound of a beaded chain clink against a glass bulb and the click of that cord being pulled. Suddenly there was light, not much, but enough to see the space around me. Nothing was down there, no bomb, just a washing machine and a dryer with a rusting lid. A pile of dirty clothes sat on the cement floor and a spider pulled himself along a dangling line of his web.

Charlie sighed. "Where is it if it's not here?"

"I don't know," Brant said, his voice sounding edgy and rough, "but we should go before someone comes home."

"Couldn't we just call the police and show them Eric's notes?"

"I don't think that'd be enough, and we'd get in trouble for being here."

We went back to school after that to get our cars. On the drive, we discussed that we were going to have to stop him tomorrow. We'd have to get to him before he set off the bomb. I hated that we were waiting until the day of to deal with him, but not knowing where he was or where he was keeping his explosives made me feel like we didn't really have any other option. I hoped that when I saw him next, I could reason with him and persuade him from blowing up the school. I think Brant was just planning to find him and tackle him before he ignited it. Whether or not we had the opportunity to talk to him or tackle him, however, was dependent on us knowing where he was planning to set the bomb off. If we could get there before him, we could stop him before he even set anything up.

We again met up later that night at my house, this time Charlie bringing with her blueprints of the entire school. All students had a map of the basic floor level, or at least had access to one to help them find their classrooms. Usually they were given out to freshmen during orientation, but what Charlie brought us was a much more detailed map that showed all storage closets and a basement layout. We sat around my dining room table, hunched over the schematic-like map, and tried to think like a murderer.

"Alright, so here's the gym," Charlie said as she drew around the rectangle of the space with a bulky yellow highlighter. The gym is where we would all be on Friday during the assembly.

"Well it's not like he's going to be setting this up beneath the bleachers," Brant said.

"Might be a little too obvious," I agreed.

"So what's the most likely place around here?"

Charlie started to highlight all the exit routes from the gym, a total of four-one at the front of the gym, another to the side and one going to each of the two locker rooms, one for girls and one for boys. "I think he's got a few options here. He could set up in one of the locker rooms, or possibly this storage closet here." She pointed to a small room on the map that wasn't in the gym but shared a wall with it. "But in both cases he'd risk having someone discover him. There shouldn't be anyone in either of the locker rooms on Friday, but that didn't mean there wouldn't be. And he'd have to carry his explosives down the halls past everyone."

"So if not the locker rooms or closet then where?"

Charlie grabbed another blueprint, this one of the basement. It was printed on a thin sheet of paper and as she laid it over the map of the main level we could see exactly which part of the basement lied beneath the gym. "Here, in the basement. Below the gym, there's a big storage unit where they keep most the sports equipment-soccer goals for the fields, those roll-y basketball hoops, that kind of stuff."

"Okay," I said, "makes sense since it's right below the gym, but won't he still have to walk past everyone with explosives to get down there?"

Charlie smiled, "That's what makes it perfect,

there's a service entrance here," she pointed again to the map, "that leads outside, and there's big metal double doors for when they have to move something big. All he would have to do is break the lock and he'd be in with easy access. This also gives him a lot more space to...well, build a bigger bomb."

As I was looking at the maps before me, things were suddenly more real than they'd ever been. It was eerie how easy this all seemed to be. It was even more unnerving, though, to think that this wasn't just a possibility, some Hollywood plot we saw in a movie. This was happening. Tomorrow morning, Eric Thompson would be filling the school basement with explosives and would try to kill us all.

"We'll have to get to school early," Brant said.

I nodded.

"If he wants to build something big enough to take out the whole gym, it'll take him some time to get it all set up."

"I vote we get there before he gets any of it put together," I said.

"Yeah, I'll second that," Charlie agreed.

Our night ended early with plans to meet on the common at six a.m. From there we would head down to the basement and intercept Eric before he could get anything put together. If I couldn't talk him out of it, Brant was prepared to take him down physically and Charlie would have her cellphone in hand to call for help. Either way, we decided, we would need to tell someone about what he had tried to do, and we couldn't risk him trying it again, but we needed to have proof first.

The rest of my night went by quietly. Both Mom and Sadie seemed to be taking Dad's absence better than they had before. We sat down together for dinner, talked, laughed, smiled. It was a happy evening. I had momentarily forgotten about the possible doom that awaited me and the rest of my classmates the following day, and for that I was glad. I needed a break, needed to spend some time with them.

Before I went to bed that night, however, the sense of worry returned. For the first time, I considered the possibility that I would confront Eric and that I would fail, that we would all fail. It was possible that Eric wouldn't listen to my words of reason, that Brant wouldn't take him out in time, that Charlie's phone call would be made in vain. It was possible that tomorrow we would all die. Thinking about it was surreal. It isn't often that one has the ability to contemplate the real possibility of their death. All I knew was that this was something I needed to do. That thought was the only thing that kept the fear from capturing my mind. Before I went up to bed that night, I hugged my mom tight and told her that I loved her, I told her that she was a good mom and that she meant the world to me. She was a little taken aback by my sudden declaration, but she laughed it off and kissed me on the forehead before heading off to bed.

Before I opened the door to my room, I was surrendered to the idea that I had a sleepless night ahead of me at best, and at worst one that was plagued with nightmares. Then I stepped into my room. With the doorknob still held in my palm, I gasped in shock and quickly shut the door behind me. Brant was in my room. He was sitting at the edge of my bed and was currently fidgeting with the small stuffed bear that I kept there. I wasn't much of a fan of stuffed animals, but the bear had been a gift from my grandfather who passed away some years back. It was one symbol of my childhood that wouldn't be easily replaced.

When he saw me, he set the teddy bear aside as if he were a small child who'd been caught playing in his father's study. For a moment, I stood in silence, still reeling from the surprise of his presence. Then the feeling of a chilly breeze brought me back to reality.

"Brant, what are you doing here?" I asked in a whispered voice. "And how did you get in here?"

"Window," he said with a shrug.

That was when I noticed that the light draft I had felt came from my bedroom window which still stood slightly ajar. The thin curtains surrounding its pane fluttered softly in the wind.

"You have a rather nice tool shed below it that was easy to climb up."

"Mom likes to garden. Why are you here?"

"I thought I'd be romantic and surprise you."

"No offense, but sneaking into my room comes off

a little more creepy and stalker-ish then romantic and sweet."

Brant stood up. "Sorry, I didn't mean to freak you out. I can go." He took a step toward the window but I moved forward and grabbed his arm to stop him.

"No, don't go... I'm not creeped out, you surprised me is all. Next time you plan to play creature of the night, just give me a heads up okay?"

He smiled. "Okay," he said then leaned in to kiss me. "So, there's going to be a next time then?" he asked when we pulled away.

I slapped his chest playfully then made my way over to my dresser to grab a pair of pajamas. "If we survive tomorrow that is." I didn't meet his eyes as I turned back around. Instead I stared intently down at my hands which held a pair of green and pink plaid pajama shorts and a grey tank top. When I finally looked up, Brant had walked over to stand before me. His hands rose to rest on my arms and he looked down at me with a comforting gaze. His hands moved up and down rubbing my arms and he smiled at me.

"Nothing bad is going to happen tomorrow, I promise."

"You can't know that."

"I know enough, we're the good guys, yeah? And, the good guys always win."

It was silly, but it made me smile and that alone was enough to raise my spirits for the time being.

Seeing my mood pick up, Brant let go of my arms and took a step away from me. "I'll, um, be over here while you change," he said, gesturing to the clothes I held in my hand.

I watched as he wandered over to the other side of the room and turned away from me to stare attentively at the photos and posters that lined my wall. It was strange, he'd seen me naked and yet it still felt comforting to have him look away for me to change. I quickly disrobed and dressed in my pajamas. The whole time, Brant hadn't so much as peeked in my direction. It wasn't until I padded toward the bed and cleared my throat that he turned back to me.

"I don't have to stay if you don't want, if you're worried about your mom, or..."

"I want you to stay, Brant."

He smiled at me and I got into bed. As I pulled my comforter up to my chin, I watched him shed his jacket and slip off his shoes. He placed the dark coat over the back of my desk chair and left the shoes beside the bed. Then he hesitated for a moment as if unsure of how comfortable he was allowed to get. After a few minutes, he mustered up some courage as he pulled off his t-shirt, setting it with his jacket, and then began to unclasp his belt.

As he undressed, I found that I was incapable of offering him the same politeness that he had offered me. My eyes seemed to be glued to the muscles of his back with every move he made. His body was lean, not a hulking mass of muscles, but fit and athletic. Then he turned back to me and my eyes darted away from his sun-kissed skin and sought out his eyes. I felt myself blush just ever so slightly but did my best to hide my embarrassment. Brant stalked toward the bed in nothing but his boxers and quickly slid beneath the covers to lie beside me.

We lied side by side for a moment, facing one another but not touching. His eyes traced the outline of my face as I took in all of his features just the same. It was almost as if we were both afraid to move anything more than the eyeballs in our heads, as if by doing so the moment we had would be lost.

"Ivy, I really do, I... I like you a lot."

I smiled. "I feel the same about you."

I scooted closer to him and his arms wrapped around me. He pulled me tight to him and kissed me softly on the forehead. His skin against mine, the heat of his body keeping me warm, it reminded me that I'm not alone. I nestled into his form.

"Brant?" I asked after a moment, my voice reverberating through the shadows.

"Yeah?"

"What did you do after your mom left?"

I felt him stiffen behind me and I worried that I'd overstepped some invisible boundary, worried that what I'd asked wasn't for me to know. Then I felt him exhale and he relaxed.

"We looked for her... at first it was just calling friends and family, then the police. Her photo was on the news, in papers, posters. We did a lot of things." He was quiet for a moment and when he spoke again, it was with a softer voice. "None of it made any difference though, we didn't find her. Didn't find any clues, no credit card receipts to tell where she may have been, didn't catch a glimpse of her on a security camera, nothing. She just vanished."

"I'm sorry."

"Don't be... maybe there's just some things we can't control... and sometimes I wonder if it's better not knowing."

I nodded into my pillow, understanding completely what he meant. Brant tightened his arms around me and within his embrace, I found the comfort I needed to find a peaceful sleep.

26

Save Me

I woke that morning at five a.m. to the screeching of my alarm clock. It startled me from sleep, but the feeling of Brant's arm wrapped around my middle quickly calmed me. As I reached toward my end table to silence my alarm, I felt his hold on me tighten, the soft hairs on his arm tickling the exposed skin between my tank top and the waistband of my shorts. I twisted around in his grasp so that I was facing him and I found his eyes open. They twinkled down at me, their lids still heavy with sleep and he smiled.

"Morning."

"We should get up," I said, my voice still sleepy and low.

"We have an hour before we need to be there."

"I need to get ready."

He frowned, "You don't need to get all dressed up to do what we need to do today."

I stared at him for a moment thinking things

over. I wanted to do nothing but lie in bed with him all day. I didn't need to kiss him, didn't need to be wrapped up in some passionate affair with him. Being beside him was enough. I resigned to stay in bed for a short while longer, but eventually did get up to shower and throw on a little makeup.

I dressed simply, in jeans and a navy V-neck t-shirt. I threw my hair up into a ponytail then left the bathroom and walked quietly back into my room. There I found Brant already dressed and waiting for me. Little conversation passed between us as I found shoes and grabbed my orange ALH zip up from my closet. Even though I wasn't actually planning to go to the assembly, I still dressed in our school colors. Partly because I didn't want to stand out, but also because they were comfy and didn't require much thought as far as planning an outfit goes. We were the Alta Ladera Eagles and our colors were burnt orange and navy blue. Those would be practically the only colors I would see that day. Except on Brant, he was dressed in varying dark shades of black and grey. That was just Brant though, I couldn't picture him in burnt orange, it wouldn't look right.

Cautiously we left my room, Brant following behind me as I peered out into the hallway to make sure that my mom wasn't up yet. She wasn't, as the house was still silent. Quietly we made our way downstairs and I left Mom a note on the kitchen counter saying I'd gone to school early to talk to one of my teachers. Then we left.

Charlie was waiting for us on the common when we arrived. She stood nervously with her arms crossed over her orange ALH tee. Brant had parked around the block from my house the night before, and he left his car there that day as we drove together in my Scion. When we parked at school, I noticed that there were few cars in the parking lot. I'd never been to school that early before and it was strange seeing it so empty, so quiet. It was like a ghost town from some old Western movie, I could even imagine tumbleweeds blowing across the sidewalk.

Once Brant and I met up with Charlie, we made our way into the school. We walked quietly side by side, watching the few students that were there pass us by. An odd kind of silence came over all of us during that short walk through the front doors and down the hall to the basement entrance. It felt as if what we were doing wasn't real. Like it was just something imagined in a dream. It felt as if I was watching the events around me on a television screen and the unnerving quiet that surrounded me was from setting it to mute. However, none of us were sleeping, we weren't watching some show. It was real, but despite knowing that, it still felt illusory.

"Ready?" Brant asked as he picked the lock to the basement door.

Wordlessly, Charlie and I glanced at one another then he opened the door and we followed him down. As I moved into the fluorescent-lit basement of the school, it felt as if I were in a trance. One foot in front of the other, stepping on dusty cement steps, my hand held the metal railing and I listened to the soft nothingness that floated through the air. If anyone else was in the basement with us, there was no sign of them.

Brant and I followed Charlie as she led us through the basement so that we were directly below the gym. We walked down a hallway where dozens of pipes created a maze above our heads, and the sound of rushing water flowed into my ears. We past a door that was marked 'Boiler Room' then made our way around a sharp corner. I saw bright blue wrestling mats stacked against the wall, and a rack of weights, bins filled with basketballs, and a gymnastic horse. My eyes rolled over every piece as I scanned the room. Then I stopped. The gym equipment, exercise bikes and baseball bats, they blurred into the background as if my eyes were the focusing lens of a camera and readjusted to look at something else. It was then that I saw him, saw it, all of it. It was that image that knocked me out of my trancelike state and back into reality. I blinked as if hoping that it all were just a mirage before me, but it didn't vanish from my sight.

In cartoons, bombs were always made of bright red sticks of dynamite and large round ticking clocks. I hadn't really expected to see anything like that down there, but I hadn't expected to see what I did either. Sometimes on TV, in spy shows, or in the movies, you see these tiny little bombs, small constructs of wire and a play-dough-like grey brick of C4 that, despite their size, seem to be able to destroy entire city blocks. This wasn't like that either. What I saw before me was a massive construct of gallon jugs that once held milk but had been emptied and refilled with an amber-colored liquid. There were wires and duct tape wrapped around the structure, spiraling from one piece to another like taffy twisting on a pull. I don't know enough about bombs to say what every piece did, but I did know that there were a lot of explosives, more than enough to destroy the school gym.

Eric Thompson was staring down at the thing he had created. I could only see the side of his face, his plump cheeks, and thick brow. His hair was greasy and black; his shoulders were hunched and brooding. He turned to us and I saw his eyes. I was expecting them to be black and empty, but they weren't. They were deep and filled with pain and confusion which seemed to visibly swirl around within his brown orbs. He looked over the three of us and for a moment I thought he looked relieved. I'd later come to realize that he wasn't looking to have someone stop him as I'd thought at the time, he wanted someone to see what he was doing because he wanted it to be known that it was him who'd done it.

It's too late, he thought.

"No, Eric, it's not too late, you don't have to do this."

His eyes darted to mine, looking surprised. He was wondering how we got in the basement, then he shook his head. "Yes, I do... I have to show them."

"Not like this. This isn't the answer."

His lips twisted into a frown and he shook his head. "Then what is?" He grew angry and I saw his plump cheeks flush red, "What will it take to make them see? Nothing."

"If nothing will make them see, then why do this?" Charlie asked.

Eric let out an agitated growl. "Because they deserve to die." His answer was cold and his words sent a shiver through me that was as cold as ice. "This isn't just about me, it's not about revenge. It's about showing them that I'm someone." His hand was fisted and he pounded it against his chest as he spoke.

"No one deserves to die like this," Brant said.

Slowly, I took a step toward Eric, my eyes steady and unmoving from his form. "Eric," I began.

"Don't, it's too late now. It's all set to go... You can't stop us."

"No, it doesn't have to be like..." My words drifted off like an echo falling away into oblivion. I paused and could feel the crease forming between my brows. *Us...* "Us?" Suddenly it rushed back to me, the voice from the library, the voice that wasn't quite Eric Thompsons. *It won't be a big enough explosion, we need more.* We, I thought, we, I had thought about that very sentence a thousand times over and never before had the word 'we' stuck out. How could I have missed that? We should never have been looking for one bomber; we should have been looking for two.

Oh God, there's two of them, Charlie thought and similar realization passed through Brant's mind.

"Eric, who else is working with you?"

"I said it doesn't matter now." *I have to do this.* Eric's eyes were back staring at his bomb like it was the accumulation of his life's work.

Ivy, we're running out of time. People are gonna start showing up in the gym soon, Brant's voice rang in my mind. He was right.

"Eric, I can't let you do this." He took a step back then and I saw him reaching for something. "Charlie, where's the most likely place for the other bomber to be?"

"Um," she said and froze.

"Charlie," I said again more firmly.

"Uh, the locker rooms... probably the boys, you'd risk running into Farrow in the girls." I watched Eric as she spoke, and saw the slight widening of his eyes.

She still won't get to him in time, I'll keep them here, he thought, and I knew that was it.

"Eric, please, there has to be something... you can't really want everyone dead."

"It's not about them... they're just a means to an end."

Again his worlds chilled me. I realized there was no reasoning with him. "Brant," I said and slowly he took a step toward Eric.

Right then, on to plan B.

Brant moved forward and Eric took another step back. He and Brant stood like that for a moment, stuck in limbo where they were both weary of the other's movement. Brant, ready to attack him and Eric, ready to dive for the trigger of his bomb in a last attempt to keep his plan from completely going under. The air was tense and thick with anticipation. We were all dominoes standing in a circle, waiting to see who would be the first to tumble and set the rest of us off into our actions. Then finally it happened.

I'm not sure who moved first, if it were Brant or if Eric had moved for the trigger to the bomb, but suddenly Brant was flying in the air and hit Eric in the chest. He wavered for a moment, unsteady on his feet. I saw him reach out toward the bomb again, but now Brant had him knocked to the floor. To my right, Charlie was dialing her phone. I looked back to Brant and saw him seemingly take the upper hand. He looked to me for a moment, just a quick glance.

"Go!" he shouted and I was off.

I think I'd been waiting for that, like a swimmer standing at the edge of the pool waiting for that gun shot. It took the sound of Brant's voice to get me to jump in, but once I was in, I was all in. I ran through the basement and raced up the stairs, taking them two at a time. I could hear Charlie behind me, she was on the phone, but it seemed that she was making her way upstairs to find immediate help as well.

None of this had gone as I had expected. I had thought it would have been easier to talk to him. I thought I could reason with him. I thought we would have gotten there before he would have had any time to set up. I had thought that there was only Eric. When I hit the hallway, I stopped for a second to orient myself and then I ran toward the gym. More students filled the halls than before. Every minute, more kids were arriving. They were going to their lockers, standing in the halls, they were in my way. I pushed past people as I moved, nearly tripping over some, but I kept going. I wasn't going to stop for anything. This was too important. I neared the door of the gym, it was only a step away, but then as it came into view, so did Tiana, Christy and Eliza.

I stopped dead in my tracks as did they. For a moment, my mind went blank. For a moment, I forgot what I was doing.

"Well look who it is," Eliza said.

"I'm surprised to see you without Brant," Christy added.

I saw Tiana look to her. *God, who cares anymore, Christy*, she thought.

"Guys," I said, "I don't have time for this right now," I tried to get past them but they wouldn't move out of the doorway.

"Jesus, Ivy, what's so important?" Christy asked. "Maybe if you spent less time running around, you'd still have friends."

I rolled my eyes then and pushed past them. As I entered the gym, however, I turned around.

"By the way, Christy, maybe if you spent less time being so self-absorbed, you'd realize that there are more important things in this world than yourself. Everyone and everything around you doesn't need to be so freaking *perfect* all the time. Maybe then you could have been there for Tiana when she needed your support, but you don't even know why she was really upset about me seeing

Brant,"

Christy looked to Ti and Ti's eyes went wide.

"Or maybe, like there's someone in the guy's locker room planning to set off a bomb and kill us all, not that anyone seems to have noticed that one but me."

"What?"

"She's not being serious," Eliza said.

"Actually, yeah, I am, you should all go, get out, and see if you can get anyone to leave with you." I turned and walked toward the locker room again.

"Wait," Christy called out to me, "Where are you going?"

"To try and stop him."

She stared at me with her mouth agape, but I turned from her and raced toward the boys' room. A moment before I walked into the locker room, I heard her think about how stupid that was; but she still didn't understand. This wasn't about me. I wasn't doing it to save me.

27

Feel the Heat

It was humid in the locker room and it smelled oddly
clean, like fresh soap. Although, considering no one
had used the locker room to change for gym yet that
day, it made sense that it would be void of the oily
smell of sweat. My shoes squeaked against the tile
floor as I walked past the showers and toward the
large open area of red lockers. Fear was making my
whole body shake. I felt like a small child that had
been locked in a closet, afraid of the sleeves of the
coats behind me as if they were monsters in the dark,
and the pounding of my fists against the closet door
was the panicked rhythm of my heartbeat. As I
walked through the locker room, my heart was
beating so hard I worried it would break my ribcage.
Then I heard a noise and held my breath, something
metal clanking against the tile and a murmured
voice. I took a deep breath and stopped walking. I
closed my eyes and calmed myself. I could do this.

I opened my eyes with a newfound sense of self-assurance and walked around the corner. There I saw him. His back was turned to me, light brown hair sitting in a mop on his head. He was hunched over, looking at what appeared to be a propane tank. Even hunched over and facing away from me, I could tell that he was tall and seemed to be fairly fit.

That should do it, I heard him think, and I knew his voice was the one that I had heard on the common and in the library.

Hearing that voice again made me angry and it helped me muster up some confidence. For a moment, I felt almost cocky, adrenaline was pumping through my veins. Adrenaline that started to flow the second I saw Eric in the basement when fear and reality had started to set in, adrenaline that had pushed me up the stairs and made me rush to the locker room. Now that adrenaline was just sitting stagnant in my veins as I stood still. It had me feeling hyper as if I were riding on a caffeine-induced sugar high. It had me feeling like I could say or do anything.

"If this were a movie, this would be that part where the villain explains his evil scheme, wasting a valuable thirty minutes of the film to tell the audience what they already know… he's just a…" he spun around at the sound of my voice, and that was when I saw his face.

He looked me over, obviously surprised to have his plan walked in on, but I was more surprised by who he was. I didn't know him personally, but I knew of him. He was the head quarterback on the football team. He was a senior with, as rumor had it, scholarships to schools all across the country. He had friends, a girlfriend, people who looked up to him. Some practically worshiped him. His life was seemingly perfect. He was Kyle Allaway.

"*You're* trying to blow up the school? But... why you?"

His eyes narrowed on me and he sighed. "You were expecting someone else? How do you even know about this?"

I ignored his second question, "I was expecting... I don't know what I was expecting, but it wasn't you. You have friends here, people that care about you, why would you want to kill them?"

Kyle scoffed. "You think because I have people around me that, what? Those people actually care about me? None of those people, none of the coaches, teachers, friends, teammates, none of them care about *me*. They care about what I can do on the field, they care that knowing me makes them more popular. I can have a dozen people around me listening to every word I say and feel more alone than any one of them. You think any of those people that float around me really agree with what I have to say? They just nod and smile because it's what they think they should be doing. They're all sheep."

"So killing them is the solution? What good does that do?"

"It will end this bullshit. The way people treat people, how I get praised like a god, but Eric gets knocked down and beat on. It's not right, not any of it."

I shook my head, none of this really making sense. There was no good that would come out of this, no one would learn, no one would be punished, they'd just be dead.

"Kyle, the only people that this is going to affect are the parents of all these students. They're the ones that are going to be hurt by this. It's not going to teach anyone here how to be better people, they'll all just be dead, what good does that do?"

"It's not about teaching them anything, it's about giving them what they deserve."

"They don't deserve this, none of them... every one of them feels the way you do. We all feel alone sometimes, we all feel like no one really cares about us. We all say bad things about other people to make ourselves feel better. Sure, it's not fair and it's not right, but we're all trying to figure out who we are. None of us know yet, so we make mistakes. We don't deserve to die for that."

He shook his head 'no,' but there was doubt in his eyes and in his mind. He wasn't sure about anything he was doing and I began to hope that I was getting through to him.

"You didn't see what they all did to him," he said in a softer voice.

"Eric?"

"They would torment him." I knew he was talking about the football players, who Eric had gym with. "Make fun of his weight, harass him physically, Ryan broke his nose when he knocked him down."

"So you're doing this for him?"

He nodded.

"Don't you see though? You didn't help him either."

"This is helping him, when everyone is gone, that will help him, and others will respect us for what we've done."

"No, you're wrong... and, you're just as bad as everyone else. You think this is helping Eric, this is going to put you and Eric in prison. Being his friend would have helped him. Standing up to the rest of the football team would have helped him. You could have stopped their bullying, but you didn't, and I know why... You don't want to be alone, it's because some of them would have looked down on you for doing the right thing, and for as alone as you feel when you have all these people around you, it's still better than being like Eric and being alone with no one."

"No, this means more..."

"This means nothing!" I shouted, and that time I knew I got through to him.

His hands reached up and tugged at his hair, pulling the light brown strands to their limit. His face contorted into a flustered and agonized expression. I watched him pace, listened to his thoughts as they flew around in his mind, one contradicting another. Then finally he came to a decision, but it wasn't the decision I'd been hoping for. His fidgety movements became solid and his eyes locked on mine. Unlike Eric's painful gaze, Kyle's eyes were a dead stare.

Then I have to die too, he thought.

Hearing him think it only gave me a second more; one more second to process what was coming. One more second to move toward the door, to make a run for it, just one more second to try and escape before he set off the bomb. My feet seemed to move on their own accord as I watched him turn. For a moment, it felt like we were moving in molasses. His hands reached out, feet twisting on cold tile floor and squeaking. I turned, my hair flipping around my head, and I ran. Again my heart was pumping so fiercely I thought it might explode. My lungs were heaving as I breathed deep. One foot, two, three…I did my best to put space behind me but I knew it wasn't enough. I rounded the corner and suddenly everything was silent. I'm sure there must have been some kind of sound. I assume explosions have a sound, but I heard nothing. I only felt the heat.

The heat propelled me forward. For a brief moment, I was floating motionless in the air, my feet off the ground. That's the last I would really remember. That feeling when you're falling and you can't catch your balance, your feet falling out from under you, arms flailing but finding nothing to grab. It's that moment of weightlessness before you hit the ground where your breath catches in your throat, all of it enhanced by the knowledge that a bomb had exploded and fiery torment was rushing my way. I remember thinking then that I was going to die.

28

All that I Am

Sometime later, someone would tell me that the bomb in the boys' locker room hadn't been as big as what was intended. It was a miracle that the explosion didn't kill me, one of my doctors would say. Kyle, however, didn't survive. Eric and Kyle had planned to have the bombs on timers. First, the basement bomb would explode. Then, as students tried to leave, the locker room bomb would go off. If anyone was still alive at that point, that is. They had brought their equipment in the night before, after the last janitor had left. That way they could move their explosives into the school in the safety of the night.

After I had left the basement, Charlie had called the police, and while I'd been trying to reason with Kyle, fire trucks had been filing into the parking lot. Brant had been able to keep Eric from doing anything until Charlie came rushing down the basement steps with Mr. Sumner and Mr. Beckman.

Eric was put in cuffs soon after that as, by that time, the police had arrived. Brant and Charlie had tried to look for me then but Christy, Tiana, and Eliza were already helping get students out of the school and they were forced to make their way outside. Brant would confess that when they all heard the bomb explode, he'd thought he'd lost me. A lot of people had thought that.

At first, I didn't remember. I woke up in the hospital not knowing how I got there or why. I had opened my eyes, squinting at first, into the bright light. I heard the beeping and whirr of machines, smelled the chemical cleanliness of the air. Eventually the memories would start to come back to me like pieces of a fractured dream, but for that waking moment, I was left with the fear of unknowing over how I got there. There was one comfort in that waking moment, however. Brant was there with me.

"Ivy," he said as I began to stir.

After that was when the panic set in as I realized where I was.

"Hey, it's okay... you're okay," he said and pulled my attention to him and away from the room.

"What happened?" I asked.

"You kind of got blown up."

I felt my eyes widen and the urge to look over every inch of my body came upon me.

"You're okay though, you're all there. There's just minor burns and you hit your head pretty hard."

That calmed me some. I still didn't remember the

explosion, but I remembered going to school that morning, remembered Eric's face, remembered the fear that I had felt.

"Where's Charlie?"

"Ah, yeah, I kind of got her grounded."

"What? Did you guys get in trouble for the bomb?"

"No... well, actually they thought I was in on it at first since they found me in the basement with Eric, but Charlie covered for me."

"So why's she grounded?"

A low chuckle escaped from Brant's lips. "Because, to explain why we were all in the basement and just happened to stumble upon Eric, I said that we had all gone down there to have a smoke."

I couldn't help but laugh. With everything we'd been through, for Charlie to get grounded because her parents thought she'd been smoking was so trivial. A few months ago, being grounded or having one of my friends grounded would have seemed like a huge burden. Now it was something I could laugh at. If Charlie getting grounded was the worst thing to happen to any of us after this, then we did alright. It was then, however, that I realized that there may have been one other thing that happened, something that would be worse than Charlie getting grounded.

Brant was looking at me, smiling at me. The expression on his face made me blush and I wondered what he was thinking. As I tried to listen in on his thoughts, I found a void where there used to be an open gate into the minds of others. There was nothing, not his voice, not any other. I was alone with my thoughts, completely. It was what I had wanted, to be free of it all, but it didn't feel that way. It felt like I had lost something that made me who I was, like I had lost a piece of me. I wondered if it was gone for good. Could I get it back? Would it return on it's own? Maybe hitting my head during the explosion had just injured my powers and maybe they would return once I healed, or maybe it had killed my powers altogether.

"What's wrong?" Brant asked.

I must have had a worried expression on my face. I quickly shook it off. "Nothing, I'm just tired, I guess. Tell me more about what happened."

Brant sat and talked with me for a long while, filling me in on everything that I'd missed. He explained his shock when he saw on the news that the other bomber had been the quarterback of the football team. He told me that a memorial service was being planned for Kyle and school had been canceled for the next week. He said that the police would probably be looking to talk to me yet and that the school was making counseling services available for all students and families. I listened to every word he said, not so much interested in the information he had for me, but just glad to hear his voice.

At some point, my parents arrived and walked in with a nurse. The nurse made it clear that Brant wasn't supposed to be there. Family only. I told her that I didn't mind but, sensing the tension he'd created with the hospital staff by sneaking into my room, and maybe to give me some alone time with my parents, Brant left.

I was glad to see my parents, and surprised to see them together, but also comforted by the fact that they were both there. It reminded me that whatever happened between them, when I needed them they would be there. Sadie was apparently being babysat by the neighbor but Mom informed me that she was anxiously waiting for me to come home. Both Mom and Dad were not only happy but relieved to see me awake. Mom had tears in her eyes as she spoke, but did her best to keep them at bay. I assured them that I was feeling okay and tried to convince them that I wouldn't have any lasting psychological damage from my ordeal but, like most parents, they were overprotective and worried about me regardless. Eventually I think it sunk in that I was alive and awake, and for the most part unharmed. By the time visiting hours came to a close, they left reassured that I would still be there in the morning.

I couldn't go home that night. They wanted to keep me for observation. That night I lay in bed for hours, staring at the ceiling. Mom had left me a few magazines in case I got bored, but it was too dark to read comfortably and not dark enough to fall asleep easily. So I just lay there, staring at the white ceiling, listening to the constant beeping of the heart monitor and the low whirr of the other machines at my sides. I'd hear the soft squeaking of a nurse's sneakers on the tile floor as she walked by my room, but I didn't hear what I was listening for. I wanted to hear someone's thoughts. The nurse outside my door, a patient down the hall, I didn't care who or what, I just wanted to hear something. Instead I led in silence, questioning if I was the same person without my ability.

Being able to hear the thoughts of others made me realize that there was more to people than what I once thought. It was what let me see the kind of people my friends really were, it was what let me see that there was a lot more to Brant than what everyone else thought. It was what allowed me to save the school from destruction, to save lives. Being able to hear people's thoughts made me grow up, it made me a better person. Would I still be that person if I'd never fallen into the Lakefall Country Club pool? Could I continue to be that person now? I didn't have any answers.

That night, I started to regret our decision to stop Eric the way we did. We should have talked to a teacher, the police. We should have passed the responsibility on. We thought we could be heroes, we thought we could be the ones to stop this. We thought that it was better to handle it ourselves for fear of others thinking we were involved, for fear of getting in trouble. Trouble was so trivial after all of this. We wanted the adventure, but it wasn't a game. I also wondered if I had done things differently that night if Kyle would have lived. The last thought that entered my mind before I finally fell asleep was wondering if I could have saved him.

A few days later, after I'd been released from the hospital and Mom had seen me up and about at home enough to be assured that I was okay, I finally got a day out with friends. It was the day of Kyle Allaway's funeral. We decided not to go. None of us had known Kyle personally and while we could see the tragedy in his death, it was still a strange concept to miss the person that had tried to kill us. We couldn't resist staying away completely, however. Perched on a hilltop across the street from the funeral home, Brant, Charlie, and I sat in the grass and watched the precession of people make their way inside.

"School starts back up in a week," Charlie said. "Think things will be different when we go back?"

"I don't know," I admitted.

"Doubt it," Brant said. "People will talk about it for a while, but eventually they'll move on from it. Life will go on as usual." He was pulling apart a flower that had been growing by his feet and I watched his fingers tear its leaves from its stem.

"It's just weird; it feels like it should change more than that."

"For some people it will."

Brant was looking on at the funeral home and I followed his gaze. Kyle Allaway's mother stood outside. She looked as if she'd walked out for a moment to get some air. She stood with her back against the brick wall and a white tissue was clenched in her hand. She hugged herself tightly and even from our distant view I could tell she was crying. This would change her whole life, and for that I was sorry. I wished that I could have saved Kyle. For a long time after that, I would dream about that day in the school and visualize all the different ways that I could have done things. Every night a different way, every night I saved him. But I hadn't really, and the truth was that I couldn't have. I felt guilty and at times I blamed myself but it wasn't really my fault. I did what I could with what I knew then. Sometimes bad things happen, I was just glad that they hadn't been worse.

That day was surreal and somber but it was good as well. That day, I saw that my friends were still my friends even without the intrigue of a murder mystery to bring us together. Brant wasn't just hanging out with me because of the weirdness of my abilities, and Charlie wasn't just spending time with us because we needed her resources. We all cared about each other as people and we were friends for no reason other than that. I had told Brant and Charlie about how my telepathy seemed to have disappeared. It wasn't something that was as interesting to them as I had thought. It didn't matter to them if I could hear their thoughts or not, it wasn't how they defined me. I realized then that it wasn't how I should define myself either. I still hoped that once my body was completely healed from the explosion that my ability might return, but I was okay if it didn't.

Brant put his arm around me and I saw Charlie look over at us and smile. For some things, you don't need to hear people's thoughts to know what they're thinking about. Sometimes you can just tell when people are thinking that they care about you.

Epilogue

The three of us took advantage of not having school that next week. On Wednesday, we went down to the beach at sunset and had a fire. Skyler and Jason joined us and the five of us sat around the warm flames talking and laughing and overall having a good time. It was a little chilly that night, so Charlie had wrapped herself up in a blanket that she grabbed out of her car and Brant lent me his coat. We all sat in the sand and watched as Skyler did impressions of various teachers at our school. He had Mr. Varnez's low lifeless tone down pat. He had us laughing hysterically.

Brant pulled me close and I snuggled into his side. I watched the orange glowing embers from the fire dance toward the sky as if they were hoping to be stars. My life was starting to feel normal again. When school did start back up, it would be just as Brant had predicted. People talked about the 'almost school bombing' for a few weeks, but then it was as if it had been forgotten.

I would soon find, however, that things weren't completely back to normal and they never would be again, but that would be okay with me. While we all laughed along with Skyler, I felt Brant's eyes on me. I glanced at him and smiled, but then my attention was pulled back to the guys and their antics. It wasn't until I heard something that I looked at him again.

I might love her, he thought and my eyes snapped to him.

My laughter fell silent on my lips and my eyes were wide. For a moment, I was frozen in surprise, surprise at what I had heard as well as the fact that I had heard it. It was a rather overwhelming moment. I was still trying to process the fact that I hadn't lost my ability when the meaning of his words occurred to me. I felt tingly all over and couldn't help but smile.

You can hear me, can't you? Brant thought.

I didn't answer aloud, but the grin on my face told him everything. He laughed and again pulled me close to him. Just then I wondered if I might love him too.

Acknowledgments

To my wonderful editor, April Tara, thank you for putting up with my horrendous grammar – and fixing it.

To all those who were beta readers for this book, it was your harsh criticisms and praises of approval, your comments, opinions and ideas of how to improve this book that made it what it is.

To all self-published authors, the wonderful stories you write have inspired me. You were the ones that showed me this was possible.

To Brandon, thank you for putting up with all the nights I spent glued to my laptop.

To Mom, thanks for everything, the support, the encouragement, thank you for standing behind me.

To all of my family and friends, thank you for being there for me and supporting my writing over the years.

About the Author

LAURYN APRIL has been writing all her life. She is currently studying Psychology at the University of Wisconsin Oshkosh; where she also lives and continues to write for young adults. You can visit her online at http://laurynapril.blogspot.com

Made in the USA
Lexington, KY
08 October 2012